DOSSIE BELL
IS DEAD

DOSSIE BELL
IS DEAD

A novel by

JACK BOONE

BRAYBREE
Publishing

Published by BrayBree Publishing Company LLC

FIRST EDITION

ISBN-13: 978-1-940127-07-1

Printed in the United States of America

BB
BRAY
BREE
BrayBree Publishing Company LLC
P.O. Box 1204
Dickson, Tennessee 37056-1204

Visit our website at www.braybreepublishing.com

To
RIDLEY WILLS II
Teacher and Friend

INTRODUCTION

Jack Boone is dead...just like Dossie Bell.

Still, it does not render him or his work irrelevant. Time has almost buried him just as Luster Holder buried Dossie Bell. The years and the march of time have swept away Boone's associates, friends, and those who inspired his writing. A professor of English and a writer, he was born in West Tennessee. It was this region that inspired his works. Indeed, his writing was confined to short stories until the publication of this novel.

It has been 80 years since *Dossie Bell Is Dead* was first published in 1939. It was a creation of its times, the hardscrabble days of the Great Depression. Like many novels of that era and similar inspiration, it contains veiled references to places and people the author knew personally. The book is set in The Tolby

Nation, a fictionalized version of The Hurst Nation, an enclave with a fearsome reputation for robbery and murder that reached into Hardeman, Chester, and McNairy counties of West Tennessee. It was named for Fielding Hurst, whose family owned much of the land within its borders. Hurst sided with the Union during the Civil War and was colonel of the Sixth Tennessee Cavalry. "The Nation," as Boone described it, closely resembled The Nation known by generations of locals growing up in those three counties. Inside that Nation and the surrounding area, Boone referred to places that possessed names identical to those actually located in north McNairy County and Chester County. These communities included Harmony, Sobby, Pilgrim's Beauty, and Refuge, as well as native features such as the Forked Deer River.[1]

In many ways, *Dossie Bell Is Dead* can be viewed as social commentary—or perhaps more appropriately a chronicle of the society—of rural West Tennessee, its people, and the times. It is commonly accepted that the novel was based on real people as well as real places. The work also serves as an astounding historical document recording many local idioms, native language, and phraseology. Many archaic traditions are chronicled in Boone's novel. The local communities portrayed are presented with both their virtues and their limitations. The reader sees the

---

1 Pilgrim's Beauty was actually Pegram's Beauty, but it was often referred to by many locals in speech as Pilgrim's Beauty.

rural communities existing around Melburg, which was Boone's fictionalized version of Henderson, Tennessee, as centered around families and clans. The importance as well as the ironies and hypocrisies of the local church and its minister is examined. The county seat served as a place of gathering for the county's country folk where they could shop, gossip, and retreat from the everyday toils of hard labor.

Neeley County—Boone's fictionalized Chester County—was a rural county where old customs were practiced by old-fashioned folks. The hills and fields of Neeley County are aptly described and little seems to escape Boone's attention as he labors to describe the countryside and its people. During the course of the novel, his portrayal of women as central to the distribution of news and the telling of events that occur in the larger community is from a viewpoint of power and strength. His exposé of the local preacher, the Reverend Lazenby, as a hypocrite whose parishioners are narrow-minded and ignorant and thus reliant upon him, is seemingly in keeping with Boone's own rather irreligious nature. In fact, Boone was not particularly religious. He was quite skeptical and sometimes derisive of his fellow citizens in and around Chester County because of their traditional evangelical views.

One must evaluate the work itself in the light of the times and the place, West Tennessee. It was a conservative time and a conservative place. The old generation and their beliefs were challenged by the likes of Jack Boone. His own morals and public attitudes had the appearance of being somewhat loose and in flux. They were not particularly fixed. Boone was given to strong drink and enjoyed challenging the local society's upper crust. He seemed far more comfortable frequenting the local roadhouses and soaking up the earthier elements of his locale. These very character traits seem to permeate *Dossie Bell Is Dead*.

At the time of its publication, the novel was controversial and raised eyebrows in and around Chester County. A review in "The Book Nook" section of the *Chester County Independent* from March 23, 1939, stated:

> Names are changed, of course. Chester becomes "Neeley" County in the book, while Henderson is "Melburg," but folks who have lived here much longer than the present reviewer (and who have swept through the book without stopping after picking it up for an experimental glance) say they recognize many a passing reference to actual happenings interwoven into the background of the book.

Indeed, this very fact led to some degree of suspicion of Boone. Small town folk in 1930s America did not like to have their limitations or their scandals exposed to public examination. Still, Boone received good reviews, even locally. While highly complimentary, the same reviewer also noted:

> There is murder in the book, matter-of-fact, almost casual murder, yet somehow it seems justice, indeed mighty close to right. Wrongs are done, wrongs are righted, there in the pines of the Nation, there in the cypress swamps. Fate closes in on the characters; each reaps as he or she has sown, and not all like the crop.

At the time of its publication, *Dossie Bell Is Dead* was frequently compared to Erskine Caldwell's *Tobacco Road*, published in 1932. The comparisons were inevitable because of superficial similarities. However, as a reviewer for *The Nashville Tennessean* on March 26, 1939, stated, "the similarity stops at the surface." According to that critic:

> The book carries no proletarian message, points no agrarian moral, expounds no cherished theory of any kind. In short, "Dossie Bell Is Dead" is that rarest of the rare: a novel without a crutch, a novel that can be read for the downright joy of it.

On Sunday, March 19, 1939, the most coveted of reviews, that found in the pages of *The New York Times*, spoke of Boone as being a young novelist "but manifestly a gifted one." The *Times* declared:

The type pattern of this novel, the restricted time the entire action takes place between the discovery of Dossie Bell's death and her funeral the following afternoon—lend it an unusual dynamic quality. Indeed it would take less tinkering than "Tobacco Road" (now running in its fifth straight year as a play on Broadway) required to make an effective play out of "Dossie Bell Is Dead."

Yet we are given half a dozen separate lives caught at one turning point or another, and any number of memorable minor scenes— Buck Humphries, cowering in the swamp, Luster Holder's revenge upon the thieves who are plundering his woodlands, a group of grandmothers dipping snuff before a cabin doorway and mulling over their ancient lore of birth and death.

Interestingly, the *Times* reviewer mentioned that *Dossie Bell Is Dead* would make a great play. In fact, an article in the June 8, 1939, edition of the *Chester County Independent* reported the novel was being considered by two New York producers for "theatrical production." Reportedly Boone and his agent in New York, Harry McGuire, had dramatized *Dossie Bell Is Dead* and reduced the action of the novel into three acts. McGuire was reported to have felt the chances were good for the work's acceptance on the New

York stage. Regardless, the novel was never turned into a play or at least one was never produced.

In fact, as the years drifted by, the novel itself seemed to drift into anonymity with Boone himself drifting but still writing and partially living off his increasingly diminishing royalty checks and his teaching salary. In 1951, the novel was republished as a paperback edition under the name *Backwoods Woman* by Dell Publishing. This publication reintroduced the novel to a new generation in a fashion far less promising than that afforded it in 1939. In fact, when the novel was first published, it appeared that Boone's prospects were bright as he enjoyed comparisons to Faulkner himself. According to the *Chester County Independent* on January 5, 1939, the novel's publisher, Frederick A. Stokes Company, a prominent New York publishing company, had contracted with Boone "for his next two novels."

Following the 1951 Dell edition of the novel, the work went unpublished again for sixty-eight years. Boone wrote other novel-length works but none were published. He continued to suffer ill health and the effects of alcoholism before dying in 1966. With his death, Boone's work and his life were further clouded by time and distance from events. He eventually became enshrouded in the erosive effects of time. His career and his health faded and the novel which came into the world of literature with such promise faded into obscurity along with its author.

Still, it never quite faded into complete obscurity. Locally, the novel remained alive in the minds and memories of a few who found the author and the circumstances compelling. A dedicated few did not forget Jack Boone even with the march of time. His life and works remained alive because of the mystery that surrounded his obscured life and the true stories behind *Dossie Bell Is Dead*. There was also the mystery about what other works could be uncovered. Indeed, Boone has mystified those who are familiar with him.

Therefore, the decision was made to introduce the man and his writings to a new generation, regardless of the scope. This 80th anniversary edition of *Dossie Bell Is Dead* was conceived as an avenue through which to reintroduce the work to older generations who grew up hearing stories about Boone and the novel as well as introduce the man and the literature to a new generations of readers. With the introduction of this novel and its concepts to a new audience comes the opportunity to unearth and publish other works written by Boone in his lifetime that were never published. There are poems, short stories, and at least one completed novel, *The Dean's Secret*, which never made their way to a reading audience.

Now, more than fifty years after his death, with the publication of this edition of *Dossie Bell Is Dead*, it is hoped that the unrealized potential of Jack Boone by and through his published and heretofore unpublished works will find an opportunity to take some root with a new audience. Every writer yearns to be read long after they are gone. Poor Jack Boone was largely forgotten before he ever died and what few published works he had were no longer in print. Perhaps it is poetically just that Boone and his works get a second chance, no matter how limited or expansive. Dossie Bell is still dead, but Jack Boone and his writings should receive a new breath of life, if just for a little while.

John E. Talbott, J.D.
Administrator
Jack Happel Boone Estate

JACK HAPPEL BOONE

———————→‡←———————

Many writers enshrouded in the veil of time and decay are mysteries to us because their lives and works are seldom visited upon their deaths. Like so many writers, some of the details of Jack Boone's life are shrouded in mystery. It appears that the mystery exists because the writer himself wrote it as such.

Two major discrepancies relate to his birth. His gravestone puts his birth as January 14, 1903. Interestingly, the sources available at the time of Boone's peak placed his birth in 1908. Of course, the information provided to the newspapers and trade papers of the day would likely have come directly from Boone and his literary agent. A review of the local newspaper coverage of *Dossie Bell Is Dead*, including the *Chester County Independent* and the *Nashville Tennessean*, show Boone's birth year as 1908. His own

Mississippi State College *Professional Personal Record*, which is in his own handwriting, lists his date of birth as January 14, 1908. Finally, the dust cover of *Dossie Bell Is Dead* states that he was born in 1908.

Why did Boone choose to pass himself off as being five years younger? Assuming the 1903 date is correct, the explanation might lie in the fact that a younger age would have established him as a younger author, hence taking off as a potential phenomenon assuming his work was successful. Such would have made him only thirty-one years old when *Dossie Bell Is Dead* was published and even younger when some of his more notable works such as "Big Singing" were published. A birth year of 1908 would have made him only twenty-four years of age when that story was published in *Household Magazine*. Being five years older would have seemed less astounding. As many writers have a shelf life with a certain window to find commercial success, perhaps Boone thought pushing forward his birth year would provide just the illusion needed to give him more time to find success. Of course, all of this is pure speculation.

The birth year is not the only ambiguity in Boone's early years. Again, his *Professional Personal Record* as completed by the author himself showed his place of birth as Trenton, Tennessee. Indeed, his family hailed from Gibson County, in the areas around Trenton and Rutherford. Interestingly, the same press and his book jacket all stated his birthplace as Clinton, Tennessee. Those same sources also claim he was a member of the venerated Boone family of which the explorer Daniel Boone was the most famous. Again, the East Tennessee birth site and the allusions to Daniel Boone may have been part of the publicity machinery to lend further credibility to an otherwise unknown writer and educator from West Tennessee.

In any event, Jack Happel Boone was born to Elbert Franklin and Martha "Mattie" Elizabeth (Ford) Boone. His father worked for First State Bank of Henderson, Tennessee, and his mother was a school teacher in the Chester County School System. Jack and his brother, Vernon Ford Boone, were very close and lifelong companions. Jack was far more serious than Vernon, but both brothers appeared to enjoy the life of eligible young men during the raucous and wide open years of the 1920s. West Tennessee abounded with roadhouses and characters of many sorts, all of which was great grist for the fiction mill. Boone's rural upbringing gave him access to stories, local folklore, interesting locales, gritty and very real characters, and a culture all its own. This background would serve Boone well as he wrote "Big Singing" (with Merle Constiner), "Dossie Bell Is Dead," "It Sure Whips Me," and numerous unpublished works.

Surviving letters between the brothers and from various parties to them indicate that both men enjoyed their social lives, were heavy drinkers, and not always financially responsible. Yet they were adventurous and found interest in the people and events surrounding them. The brothers were especially close and ideas for Jack's writing abounded in their environs. Vernon worked sporatically for John F. O'Neal & Company, a Henderson general merchandise firm, most of the years that Jack was teaching and writing. Vernon himself wanted to write and penned one unpublished short story that survives, *Test of Hate.* Despite his own interest in Jack's craft, Vernon never stopped trying to supply Jack with material for his efforts. His letters to Jack were full of information and ideas.

The world these brothers knew was right out of a novel or short story of the 1920s and 1930s. They knew a rural countryside with dirt roads and rustic, backwards people who were not far removed from the ways and traditions of their ancestors. Their friends and associates included other young men who yearned for adventure and spent nights fighting, drinking, carousing, and stirring up the dust along the back roads and pig paths of West Tennessee. They knew people who drank too much and men who ran whiskey stills and carried on commerce in the deepest of the region's woods. There were young women who were rebelling against their strict upbringing by running around with reckless young men like the Boone brothers and declaring their feelings and fears in night time letters written to them. There were joints and roadhouses full of characters whose very existence gave Jack Boone a wealth of information from which to mine.

Jack attended Memphis State College and Vanderbilt University, where he earned his Bachelor of Arts Degree in 1930. He remained at Vanderbilt for his graduate studies, earning a teaching fellowship and his Masters of Arts Degree a year later while working towards his Ph.D. Studying English in both programs, he was preparing for a life in which words could have been central and indeed often were.

The decade of the 1930s was an active period for Boone. From 1932 through 1935, he wrote for several newspapers and magazines as a freelancer. It was during this period that he collaborated with Merle Constiner, later a successful writer of western fiction, and lent his talents to several publications. He wrote for Street & Smith Publications of New York, Methodist Publishing Company, Baptist Publishing Company, *Household Magazine*, and *Story Magazine*.

Boone and his friend Merle Constiner co-wrote the short story "Big Singing," set in the hills of rural Tennessee, that was published in *Household Magazine* in 1932. The quality of the story was such that it was reprinted in the O. Henry Memorial Volume of Prize Stories for 1932. A column in the *Chester County Independent* on November 3, 1932, mentioned that "several well-known magazines have carried Boone-

Constiner stories in the past two years."[1] According to *The Nashville Tennessean*, in its March 26, 1939 edition, Boone had also published short stories in such nationally known magazine and journals as *Prairie Schooner*, *Midland*, *Haldeman Julius Monthly*, *Southern Review*, and *Star Detective*.

Between writing and teaching, Boone remained busy throughout the decade. In 1936, he wrote the short story "It Sure Whips Me" that made O'Brien's Roll of Honor, The Best Short Stories of 1937. He wrote regularly for magazines and newspapers from 1932 until 1935. In 1935, Boone became Editor-in-Chief for a New Deal initiative called the Federal Writers Project for Tennessee. His tenure was turbulent, however, and by 1938, prior to the actual publication of the *Tennessee Guide*, Boone had resigned. Thereafter, he became an instructor in English at Clemson College (now Clemson University) in South Carolina. He remained there for a year before joining the University of Iowa as an instructor in the short story. Boone left that position to return to South Carolina and serve as an assistant professor of English at Presbyterian College. He taught there from 1940 until 1942, while also working as an associate editor for Jacobs Press in Clinton, South Carolina. From 1943 to 1944, he served as an instructor in English at Georgia Tech. Then in 1944, he went

---

1 The possibility of other stories by the duo is plausible and likely and so a little literary archaeology may yet yield more long buried treasures. At least two unpublished novels exist. Other short stories long ago forgotten with time would add to the treasury of known Boone literature.

north to teach as an assistant professor of English at Rensselaer Polytechnic Institute in Troy, New York. Boone began teaching at Mississippi State College in Starkville, Mississippi, in 1949. Unfortunately wherever he taught, it seemed that controversy inevitably followed.

Throughout his college teaching career from 1938 until the early 1950s, Boone continued writing though his success was limited. His alcoholism worsened and his health began to decline in the early to mid-1950s. He wrote one novel during this period, *The Dean's Secret*, a parody about American college academia. It was submitted to his agent, A.L. Fierst, of New York City, but Boone never saw it published. According to Boone's own notes, he was at work in 1949 on a novel set in the period of 1878–1880. Whether this novel was ever completed is not known. In 1951, *Dossie Bell Is Dead* had been republished as a paperback by Dell Publishing under the name *Backwoods Woman*. Perhaps this new edition allowed continued—although surely limited—royalties.

By 1956, Boone's career had so faded that he was employed in St. Louis, Missouri, by the public school system as a substitute teacher, a long descent from his collegiate career. He was also frequently hospitalized and spent considerable time in Alexis Brothers Hospital following a stroke. Other sources have stated that he suffered from tuberculosis. He lived at the YMCA in St. Louis and corresponded frequently with Vernon and his mother, who was then residing in the Luckett Rest Home in Gibson County, Tennessee.

In the last decade of his life, Boone's health and fortunes continued to decline. He eventually returned to Henderson, Tennessee, after suffering the stroke in 1956. His last ten years were spent in retirement and largely writing. He had been a character himself in youth but age and ill health seemed to rob him of his vitality. Boone died of a sudden heart attack at his home in Henderson on Saturday, April 23, 1966. He was buried at China Grove Cemetery in Gibson County, Tennessee. He was survived by his brother Vernon and a host of cousins and other extended relatives.

In short, Jack Boone's life was interesting but his career was stifled by that life. He experienced frustration in both his academic and writing careers. He was beset by some of the same problems that many prominent writers experienced. The writer Donald Davidson, a prominent member of The Fugitives, once warned him about the dangers that excessive alcohol use could pose to a writer's career. Boone's life was turbulent and it appears his relations with co-workers and especially his academic superiors suffered as a result. That his career never reached its potential was predictable with the powers of retrospect.

Jack's brother, Vernon F. Boone, was his closest companion during his ill-fated life. Vernon was a wandering soul himself who drank too heavily, indulged in little more than a subsistence life and indulging his past times. Both Jack and Vernon lived through and enjoyed the days of the local bawdy house, road house, and speakeasy. They both engaged in affairs with smart, liberated young women and seemed to expend their best years in the throes of alcoholism. They wrote to one another frequently and shared ideas, most of which never came into fruition. Ultimately, the brothers were joined in death within a short time of one another, Vernon following Jack in 1967. The brothers are buried side by side at China Grove Cemetery.

Jack Boone is long dead, but perhaps his works and his legacy may receive a new breath of life—a second chance, something perhaps even he would never have imagined. Publishing his greatest work *Dossie Bell is Dead* for the first time in 68 years is the initial step in that revival.

FOREWORD

———— ►‡◄ ————

I**T'S HARD TO KNOW** just what to say in writing a
Foreword about Dossie Bell and West Tennessee.
Few things that concern this section of Tennessee
have been written in fiction. Even the rest of the
state feigns ignorance when the western part is mentioned. The old Western District is as foreign to the
average East Tennessee mountaineer as the salt flats
of Utah—hundred of winding miles lie between
Hangover Mountain and Reelfoot Lake. And the
Middle Tennessean refers to the Mississippi River
section as "that swamp."

But West Tennessee, like the other two divisions
of the state, has its hills, and in addition its lakes and
bottomlands. This region, the last frontier of the
state, lies between the Tennessee River on the east
and the Mississippi on the west. There are rugged

hills, rolling highlands, rich flat bottomlands, and the heart of the Chickasaw Nation, and after the French and Spanish were replused in their efforts to take it, the Chickasaw ceded it to the United States. In the central counties lived John A. Murrell, the murderous horse-and-negro thief of the Natchez Trace. David Crockett settled in the northern portion and killed hundreds of bear around Reelfoot Lake. Natah Bedford Forrest led his gray-men into every West Tennessee quarter during the Civil War.

Even today much of the spirit of the frontier prevails, and many of the descendants of the earliest settlers have Chickasaw and Cherokee blood in their veins. This folk, which akin to the East Tennessee mountaineers, still retain a wester, roving spirit.

The primitive conditions described in this book still hold to a great extent in the back-reaches of hill and river-lands. The people described live in the wooded hills, where it is hard to grow substantial crops, or in the bottoms adjacent to the streams, where crops are often washed out by raging floods. In pre-prohibition days many of this folk lived off the liquor they distilled and sold. And they were ready to kill to protect their rights. They are for the most part sharecropper, moonshiner, and swamp, or river-rat, types. Since the New Deal a large number have moved to the small towns and taken relief jobs, for the new government whisky has caused charred corn to be scarce.

I came to know West Tennessee because I was born there and lived all over the place. When the educated town people failed to hold any magic for me, I turned to the hillmen. In these people I found a quality old and unveneered. For some reason, the "tough, unreliable crowd." seemed to accept me as one of its own. In fact, grimly, out of the past, I was one of them. In their way of life was something strengthening—the utter leisureness and indifference of it to outward change. The don't-give-a-damn spirit appealed to me.

I met my Luster Holders and Squire Kilers, whether over kegs in the deep wood or under hickories by the open doors of windswept churchhouses in which the Brother Lazenbys talked confidently of that most certain consuming hellfire—a child's toy-match conflagration to the Lusters and the Squires. I came to admire them and to write of them in short stories. "Dossie Bell," which appeared in the Prairie Schooner. I liked the characters. They suggested to me the possibility of a long work. I wished to develop them and their "country"--that's what they call it. The product is the present book. And although it deals with the back beyond class I have known, actually I do not portray any person living or dead.

JACK BOONE

Clemson College, S.C.
January, 1939

DOSSIE BELL
IS DEAD

1

As the man shouldered his way through the thick Saturday crowd silence fell over the hot summer day. Folks watched him, the tall leathery man in faded denims. They saw the dead-set of his oily gray eyes, how he moved among the intermingled town and hill folks as if he alone existed. He seemed searching for something without actually looking. There was a soft animal tread to his walk.

Melburg was overflowing for trade day: country folk wedged around the drygoods stores and groceries to make the sidewalks all but impassable. Women with small children swinging to their hands or babies astride their hips stood talking self-consciously. Young girls, arm in arm, giggling, paraded back and forth in front of Tart Nelson's poolroom so the boys and men could see their new calicoes,

ginghams and silks—so that some of the boys would
finally break from their set and take them driving
to the woods. Hillmen on the street-corners dis-
cussed crops, argued religion or politics, or court,
which was in session. Others loitered at Lucket's Beer
Palace and mixed corn whisky with their brew. The
torpid heat-waves seemed to melt the blues and reds
and yellows of overalls and dresses. The colors ran
together in a crazy quilt liquid.

All talk and bustle ceased as the man passed. The
crowd parted for him as if sliced with a knife. People
whirled from their circles to stare, mouths gaping
open as if his eyes had caught them in the full open-
ness of speech and frozen them there. Everybody
knew him and pointed behind his back. His reputation had reached them in the remotest corners of
Neeley County. It had come in increasing waves of
gossip over the red-clay hills.

"It's Luster Holder. He's Indian. Better leave
him be."

"You spit a mouthful, hoss. He'd kill you for a
quarter and give you twenty cents back in change."

If he noticed them, no one knew. They watched
his lank form disappear down the street. But in memory they could still see his sunken eyes, the black
hair low across his forehead in cutacross bangs, the
sinister slope of his broad shoulders.

His passing threw a pall over those who saw him.
They knew Luster Holder well. He seldom came out
of the West Neeley hills. He lived in the Old Tolby

Nation and owned most of the land. No one settled near him. He lived in a small cabin with a woman he had never married. There were many tales of how he had kept outlanders from his country; of how he fought any fashion and clove to no law but his own. None of the Saturday throng had forgotten the Marston killing: Lide Marston had been found, choked to death, in the sedgegrass of a creek-washed ravine near Firbank. Two officers had driven out of Melburg one rainy April afternoon and headed toward the West Neeley hills. They returned three days later on foot, muddy, scratched and bleeding from their long walk. They never explained anything, nor were they candidates for re-election.

Nothing was ever done about this lawlessness. Melburgers were stirred up, but there was no investigation. Whispered reports from Firbank said, "Luster Holder." It was never proved. He distilled whisky and sold it by the hundred gallons. No move had ever been made by the county law to stop him.

"I wonder what he's up to over here?" a sharecropper in rubber boots asked.

A stooped Hillman still held his watery eyes to the spot where Holder had disappeared. "Hain't no good, I warrant you, Obie."

"I wonder does the law know he's in Melburg."

"Shucks, them laws hain't itchin' to know about him. They hain't so dumb. They'd tuck their tails and take out if they got the least suspicion."

"I figger he's brung Tart Nelson some of that 'ere chartered stuff. Tart's the only feller over here he'll talk to. They say Tart done him a favor wonst."

The sharecropper shook his head gravely.

"Was I Tart I wouldn't be too loose with that 'ere Cherokee. He's liable to wake up early some bright mornin' with his throat cut from year to year."

Luster descended a steep ridge and entered the valley. He paused and swung the heavy sack of flour from his shoulder. He looked at the semicircle of hills which rose about him. A little while ago the sun had gone down behind them like a red thumb-smear. Now they lay in a low crescent of smoky cobalt like blue hounddogs in repose.

He was very tired. His back had begun to bend in increasing ache. His blue denim jumper was hot and sweaty, rubbing hard and stiff against damp shoulders.

He watched the half-light of evening fall over the valley; then fade into gray-silver, the false after-illumination which just precedes the summer dark. The listless trees hemmed in the valley and cut it out distinctly from the world back there at Melburg. This isolation was restful to the man. He thought of Melburg and was for a moment lifted back to the crowded streets, the movement and noise. He had gone there for a forty-eight-pound sack of flour. Dossie Bell liked the Tennessee Rose brand best and the Forbes Store at the county seat was the only one to handle it.

He was glad to be nearing home. Among this wild sweep of hovering hills he felt something seeping into him, a soothing power which they always gave. To him, the trees, the ragged ridges, were living.

His brow clouded at a recollection: somebody had been cutting trees in his lower wood beyond the creek. Wurner Crouse had told him yesterday and he hadn't had time to investigate. He would see about it after he'd slept a good night's sleep.

He reshouldered his flour and crossed the soft grassland. He walked along the hillside, through the stony sheep pasture, toward the springhouse. He picked his steps carefully as he walked. In places the pasture was rough: here and there the thin topsoil had washed away to spot the land with brown sandstone; there were prickly pears—known as mule-ears—cowitch vine, bull-nettle, tickle-grass, boneset weed and dog-fennel.

Farther on, the pasture was cut deep with jagged red gulleys: the bad-lands: dangerous for stock if they wandered too close and the ground crumbled.

The springhouse was down in the corner of the pasture near the wagon-gate: a decaying log shed built over a tiled spring. The water bubbled up from low down in moving white sand and overflowed in a sparkling stream at the top, oozing over the rim of the tile as if cautiously pushed up from far down in the earth. A clump of five old cedars spread their dark-green ragged limbs above the roof and helped keep the place isolated from the torpidity of the summer air.

Luster Holder entered the springhouse and eased the sack of flour to the damp earth. He stooped by the spring, his knees sinking into velvety moss, and for a moment saw his burnt-brown face reflected like himself, only darker, on the round, glass-clear surface.

He hadn't come by the springhouse for water. He had told his woman to suspend four bottles of brew in the spring. She would tie a piece of hemp string around the necks of the bottles and stake it in the soft earth. He would stop by for them on his way back from town. He knew the long walk with the heavy sack would tire him and he would need refreshing. He sure liked homebrew. These four bottles had been chilling since morning and would be good. Climbing and descending hills, wading the creek and cutting across fields tired a fellow so he needed the foamy liquid to work through his body and ease him back into the man he had been before he started out.

The beer would be there: Dossie Bell had never failed to do what he requested. The power of the four bottles would build an appetite for the good supper she would have waiting for him—whippoor-will peas, fried ham, buttermilk, green tomato pickles, cold corndodgers and peach-cobbler. She knew just what he liked. She would sit opposite him at the table, attentive to his every need, asking questions in her quieting way.

His stinging, sun-blinded eyes searched below the water surface. There was no homebrew in the spring; just the usual can of cream and Mason-jar of buttermilk.

Luster was bewildered. He had walked most of the afternoon. The hot, brilliant sunlight had dulled his mind, and hill climbing in his hard brogan shoes had numbed his whole body.

In the rattling black cedars, above his head, birds were scrambling into silence.

She had forgot the homebrew. He couldn't figure it out. He'd told her just before he left the house, "Put three or four bottle of brew in the spring, Dossie Bell. I'll drop by for them on my way home." But she hadn't. She had failed him for the first time since he had taken her to his cabin to live with him. There must be a sound reason for her forgetfulness. His mind was too slowed down to make it out.

He was ready to drop. The weight of the flour had gradually edged into his joints and stiffened them. It had become like some growing misery of which he couldn't be shed.

Again his pale eyes searched the spring, unbelieving. He got to his feet and lifted the flour to his shoulder. Still thinking brokenly, he started for the cabin.

A path led in a direct line to the house. Crabgrass and jimsonweed, bordering it, were already wet from the early evening dewfall. Night was coming on like dropping soot before the eyes of the big hillman. A breeze from the direction of the fallen sun talked droningly into his ears, cooling and drying the sweat on his face into a salty stiffness.

He threw one leg over a rotting rail fence. He paused to try and get everything to come clear to him. Why had Dossie Bell failed him? It wasn't her way. She was a woman on whom one could always depend.

Luster's cabin lay far back in the hills of Neeley County—the heart of the Nation country of West Tennessee. This sparsely settled section was called the Nation because the Tolbys had come into it back in the early days of the western district and gunned anyone who tried to follow them. The Chickasaw Indians had relinquished the country to the state a short time before. It was possible for a man to step out at his back door and lose himself among dense trees from which hung impenetrable muscadine and wildgrape vines. To make a trail he must tear through stubby hazelnut and clinging blackberry bushes. Deer, bear and wild turkey made food plentiful.

During the Civil War General Artie Tolby had organized a Yankee company of scalawags, cutthroats, bushwhackers and thieves. They did no real fighting but preyed on the Confederates, robbing and killing. It was well known in Neeley County how Luster's grandfather had come into the Nation and run the Tolbys out. John Holder was a Cherokee Indian who settled in Neeley County with his white wife. He had been the first to throw fear into the Tolby clan. Working alone, he harried General Tolby's forces: playing on the outskirts of the company, he killed stragglers, overpowered pickets and carried off horses. He brought home as many as twenty horses at a time. He cut off his victims' ears and, when he had collected a batch, sent them to General Tolby. Following the war he and his three sons had barred the Tolbys in their Cedar Hill home, set fire to the house, and shot Tolbys one at a time, leisurely, as they sought to escape. Wounded in the fight, John had done most of his shooting from the ground.

He broke up the Tolby clan. General Artie Tolby had moved to the edge of the hill country, nearer Melburg. Here he had waited with his relatives for a chance to regain their lost lands and gun the Holders from the state—a chance which was still swinging.

Luster had inherited over a thousand acres and no one in West Tennessee questioned his right to it.

The weary hillman approached the cabin. It was three-roomed: a narrow house with a slanting tin roof. The two front rooms were separated by an open hall—the dog-run. The outer walls were covered with broad whitewashed planks. At the side of the cabin was a tall hickory which sent crooked limbs out over the roof. Where the leaves had dripped water onto it, the tin was snuff-brown. In front of the dog-run were three cedar trees. From the cabin, hills stretched in falling rolls of green until they rose again and disappeared in the distant haze, seeming to melt away with the sky.

Packer and Hobart, Luster's possum and coon dogs ran to meet him, barking and prancing at his knees. They were heavy-shouldered dogs with flapping ears. Packer was yellow-brown, while his partner was mixed brown and black. Luster paid them no mind. Usually Dossie Bell would be standing in the runway awaiting him.

No lights were in the cabin. Dossie Bell hadn't lighted a lamp. Luster walked down the dog-run. She must be in the kitchen preparing supper. Possibly she was out in the chicken-yard feeding the chickens and barring them up for the night. He couldn't understand why she had forgotten the homebrew.

"Dossie Bell, where you at, Dossie Bell?"

She must be down at the barn shelling corn for the hens. She always filled a bucket with corn for next morning.

Luster walked through the big-room where there were a four-poster bed and brick fireplace. In the kitchen he paused to take a drink of water from a cedar bucket. Where could Dossie Bell be? He was tired and hungry. No fire had been kindled in the kitchen stove.

He put the flour in the pantry bin. He looked from the window toward the gray shack of a barn. No one was in sight. He returned to the big-room.

A rocking-chair was near the north window. He let his body bend in a half motion toward the chair. His eyes rested on the bed. Dossie Bell was stretched across it.

"Dossie Bell! Dossie Bell!" he called wearily.

She slept on. Luster walked to the bed and studied her motionless form, sunk deep in the warming featherbed. He shook her. Dossie Bell didn't move. He looked at her a moment, puzzled. He stooped over and shook her again. He lifted one of her hands which hung over the edge of the bed. It was cold.

He pulled off his hat and ran a hand through his straight black hair. For minutes he stood, slow wonder treading his mind. He reached down and let the center of his palm rest on her forehead. It was cold. He put his ear to her breast. There was no sound.

Luster backed from the bed. Still backing, he let himself sink into the chair. He stooped over and began unlacing his shoes. His feet hurt and his dull gray eyes stung like hell. His back was very tired.

Dossie Bell was cold and dead. She hadn't put the homebrew in the springhouse because she was dead. It came slowly, ceaselessly, to a mind befogged.

The rocking-chair was easy to Luster's back. He sat while darkness erased the objects in the room. All was silent to his mind. The hollowness of silence dwelt in the swirling black, coming in from the hills. The wind did cry down the mud-daubed chimney, this only adding to the quiet gloom.

Minutes passed before he moved. He stretched himself from the chair and wound the tall clock in the center of the mantel. It was seven fifty-four. He looked from the window. The night was hot. The big hillman emerged from his mind-silence and for the first time collected to knowing the noises of the night: Balky, the Jersey cow, was lowing by her trough in the mule-lot. Dossie Bell hadn't milked her. Cooter and Carnes, the gray mules had to be fed. Pattie Pide, Dossie Bell's heifer, was about ready to calf: she needed seeing after.

Frogs kept up a dismal chorus in the pond back of the barn. Katydids and July flies grated at each other monotonously from tree to tree. Packer and Hobart growled low in their throats at straying stock.

Luster walked to the kitchen and took a quart bottle of liquor from the stovewood box. He poured a water-glass half-full and drank it. With the bottle in his hand he returned to the room where Dossie Bell lay dead.

Something had to be done. Dossie Bell was up and all right when he left her early in the morning. Drawn between the usual duties and the presence of death, Luster sat down again. He was confronted by a never-before-known problem. But with the pleasant burn of the whisky in his veins his mind couldn't stay in the present. In its tired state there surged up the mixed memories of days and days.

He remembered when he first met Dossie Bell. It was at church over on McHaney's Ridge. She was

there alone to hear the Nazarene minister's last sermon at Big Meeting. She sat by herself to one side
of the house, a small, timid, girl-woman with melty
brown eyes which looked much too big. It was the
look of aloneness more than her beauty which took
him in. He'd thought at the time, "She shore hain't
bin took much good keer of where she's bin at." He
didn't like at all the way some of the women and girls
pointed and whispered.

She lingered behind after services broke. A group
of men and boys stood under a hickory in front of
the church, waiting to see where the strange woman
was going.

When Luster approached her, she didn't move;
her eyes were held up to him like a small child's,
searching, and even then trusting. He saw that she
was very young.

"Are you out here by yourself?" he asked.

"Yes, sir."

"Where you live at?"

She lowered her head. "I ain't got no reg'lar place.
My folks has turned agin me. I been stayin' at Ole
Auntie Gates, the nigger which has a cabin over on
Cleeburn Creek."

He didn't ask her anything else.

"You come with me to my cabin," he said solemnly. "You kin stay there."

Without a word she followed him through the
thick woods. He pushed vines and bushes from their
faces. The moon was in a spun cocoon of clouds. Its

pale orange beams scarcely penetrated through dark oak and hickory leaves.

And she had lived with him as his woman while people condemned her. The church-folks banded against her even though she had gone to church faithfully. They turned her out at Sobby while Old Man Henley Humphries fought to keep her name on the book. Brother Lazenby, the pastor, said it was best. Her soul would never be clean, he said, until she left Luster and came on bended knees to ask forgiveness of the Nazarenes. Brother Lazenby had worked to get her to do this. He had worked with caution.

Luster heard of the talk, the church stir. He never mentioned it to Dossie Bell. He knew she was hurt, for she loved her God. Folks' talk never bothered him.

All of these gone-things returned to Luster soothingly. He sat in a languorous state reviewing them. It was as if his woman's death had suddenly ended his own forward going. She would be hard to replace. Women like Dossie Bell didn't happen around every week day.

He strained from his chair. He pulled on his shoes and stood. His woman was dead. When a body died on you, you had to see other folks. You had to get them to sit up and take care of the corpse. This was usual. He didn't see any need of sitting up with the dead. When a body died, he could be harmed no more.

He figured on it laboriously. "I could be here with her and see to her all she needed 'cause she hain't gonna be needin' nothin' now. Me and her never keered for nobody round us when she was up and breathin'. But maybe hit would be best to let folks know. They'll be wantin' to be over here a-seein' and a-doin'. Bein' dead's something else. Hit ain't for you to be pleased. She's the one. She'd about like for some of them folks which churched her to come over. She never seemed to hold nothin' a-tall agin them. Hit ain't for me to say what's right for the dead. I'll git them over like others does when they's a dyin'. I'll do hit for her. She'd want hit that-a-way, and I hain't givin' a damn myself."

He was faced with death for the first time, natural death. He had seen men killed, but he never thought of them as actually dying. They had been wiped out and through with. Dossie Bell had been up and well when he left for Melburg. He couldn't get it straight how something had taken her off so suddenly.

Luke Tolby was Luster's nearest neighbor. Luke lived by himself just the other side of Cleeburn Creek. Luke was the last of the Tolby menfolks, the once powerful Tolbys whose very name was a legend with the hillfolks. He lived five miles east of Luster's, on the last high ridge before the land sloped down to the Forked Deer bottom country. Luster knew a short-cut through the woods to Luke's house.

"He's the nighest which lives close to me," he figured. "Ole Luke may kin tell me the best thing to do. He's had folks die round him."

The cutacross to Luke's was over hard country—pastures, hillsides, hollows, briars, newground, brush.

Luster started out. He was tired at first, but his muscles limbered up. The night was sweltering. The moon was shining off and on, a white water-ring wide around it. Night made the country strange, new, unknown.

He took an old wagontrack through the hills. He sweated like a work-mule. Even at this height there was no breeze. The oak leaves above his head were rigid and motionless. He panted up the hillside.

A flash of heat lightning cut the leaves out in green ice. After the flash it was very black and climbing was difficult. The lightning continued intermittently: silver-green, black. With each flash he could see his path magnified before him. He was careful to watch out for bad vines and briars: he knew the country well. With each black blotting out he was left plunging onward in a common darkness.

By the time he climbed to the ridge, the sky had clouded and there was the smell of rain in the air. A different kind of lightning danced helter-skelter in the north; it ran down the sky, arching like rivulets of butter beyond the clustered crests of the hills. A breeze cooled Luster's armpits.

The rain passed over, moonlight again breaking through.

"We shore need hit," he thought. "If hit would just rain, we'd have a season."

He walked along the ridge until he came to a dry stream and then started the descent. The stream had a shale bottom and the flat stones slid beneath his shoes. He wished he had brought his gun: there were bobcats in these woods. "I'd shore like to bring down another one of them boogers," he said aloud. "I git tard hearin' them scream way out some'rs at night. They cry like a skairt woman." His voice sounded dry, cracked.

The red-clay gulley became deeper. The cut was even with Luster's shoulders. The dusty smell of dry sod rose to his nostrils. He stamped through reefs of drift, pipestem weeds cracking and popping noisily. He stopped to roll a cigarette and found he had left his paper at home—he'd forgot to tear off a piece of brown sackpaper when he was in the kitchen.

At last he reached the ridge where Luke lived. He paused at the highest point. Far away below him, where the foliage left an opening, he could see the backwaters like silver stirred in among the black tree-trunks.

He watched for minutes, breathing in deeply of the singing air. He felt thirsty and hoped Luke had a drink.

2

LUSTER FOUND LUKE TOLBY in the kitchen. Tolby was sitting near a small oil-lamp which gave out a faint yellow light through its smoke-blackened chimney. He was oiling a shotgun which lay across his knees.

He raised his head as Luster entered. Slow surprise filled his mud-brown eyes. His long legs were spread far in front of him. His dark face was in a perpetual scowl, the lines of the sensually brutal mouth carved as if in red clay; the stubby nose a bruised purple. He sat naked, the hairs on his chest like a thick black mat. Sweat ran from his forehead and fell onto broad slanting shoulders in big drops which burst and scattered wetly against his arms.

"Hidy, Luster," he said with forced gruffness, not rising. In the gruffness was hard-to-hide respect. He was thinking, "I wonder what's brung him over here. I disremember if he's ever bin before."

"Hidy, Luke."

"Have a cheer. I figger I'm like to common." Luke veered his eyes from the tall Holder man. He studied the shining blue-steel of the gun-barrel.

"I hain't got no time to set down, Luke. I wanted to see you."

Tolby lowered his head and was again busy at his oiling, seemingly unconcerned. He raised his gun and slanted one eye through the barrel. He lowered it and began rubbing it off with an old piece of union-suit.

"Luke, Dossie Bell's dead."

"Did which?"

"I say, Dossie Bell's dead. She's heerd her Maker's horn."

"How come, Luster? Who killed her?"

"I found her across the bed cold as pond ice. I hain't got no idear what takened her off. She allus did have a misery in her heart."

"Wull, I be goddam! Whoever heerd tell of anything to beat hit? What you 'low you'll do?"

Tolby tried the breech-lock and broke the gun, taking another quick glance through the barrel.

"Shore bad her takin' out on you this time of year," he added. "Hit's the busy season too." (Thinking: "I wisht he'd git on now. He talks about Dossie dyin' like I would a hoss or hawg. There 'ere devil-quiet way of his'n plumb fizzle-springs me.")

"Yeh, I hain't shore what to do."

"I figger you'd better git Preacher Lazenby. He's a good hand with the sick. He'll know what to do. I'd go with you myself, but I got to be watchin' round here."

"Something wrong?"

"Bode Holley he stole a ten-gallon kaig of licker from me the other night. He hepped with the run and was the only one knowed whur hit was buried at. He got drunk and sold some at the store. He's lowratin' lies on me."

Luster listened without comment.

Luke continued, "You recollec' when we cleaned off the graveyard over to Refuge? He's tellin' I didn't put in my time. He's sayin' I color my whisky with snuff. Thar never was no bigger lies said nowhar. He's bin gittin' licker-brave at the store and sayin' he's gonna run me outen the county. That's bin words which brought on one thing and then two. I'm ready to pay up."

Luster's eyes were on Luke's rounded shoulders.

"Wull, you know thar hain't never no Tolby never tole no lie. I'm gonna blow hell outen him first time I lay eyes on him. A short hoss is easy curried."

He waited for Luster to say something, then went on. "Hit's me or him now, Luster. I've stood all any man kin stand. 'y God, Luster, I bet he's one of them which is in that 'ere wood thieve bunch. They've takened several big cypress offen my bottomland. Have you missed any?"

Luster moved toward the door. "No, I hain't, Luke. Guess I better be gittin' on. I'll see Brother Lazenby. I figger Dossie Bell would want a preacher in the house, her bein' a Christian and all. Hit must be about three miles from here to his house. I want a drink fore I go."

Luke brought a gallon jug from under the bed. Luster titled it on his arm and drank.

Luke said, " I 'low the preacher'll know right short off what to do. By the way, Luster, fore you go, have you heerd my niece Birdie Kiler's in a fambly way?"

"No, I hain't, Luke."

Luster's gray, changeless eyes worried Luke. "I wisht I hadn't started in to tell him. I jest thought I'd feel him out on hit. He fusterates me hellaciously. He sees through a feller. He looks in yore insides and sees the color of yore guts."

"Hit's that damn Buck Humphires," he said unevenly. "He's ruint sister Millie's gal. Squar Kiler's goin' out to hunt fer him tonight. He's got to marry her. We'uns cain't offord to let no sissy young whelp like him ruin our gals." He raised sullen eyes to the standing man.

"I figger not, Luke." I'd hep the Squar mysef if I wasn't so bore down with my own troubles."

"I better be gittin' on to the preacher's."

Luster stepped back into the night. It hugged up around him in a hot blanket of darkness. Over the ridge, faintly, he could hear the barking of his hounddogs.

"They're tryin' to tell ever'body Dossie Bell's went away," he thought glumly. "You cain't fool dogs. They know and feel more than folks does."

He thought of what Luke told him. Luke sure better keep his eyes out for Bode Holley. Bode had the name of being a sneaking coward who never did anybody good. He had hidden behind the Firbank schoolhouse one night and lain for old man Pole Bradley. When Pole came by, Bode lunged and cut him badly. The Holleys were bushwhackers. But Luke Tolby was a man who managed to take care of himself fairly well. Not many had the nerve to tamper with him. Luke might be the last of the Tolby men-folks, but he was as all-fired mean as the first ones, Old Artie included. Luster recalled his grandfather, John Holder: how he had got possession of the Nation lands. He could shore use a gun and play a fiddle.

Luke's niece, Birdie Kiler, was in trouble. It was hard to believe a boy like Buck Humphries was to blame. Buck was too shy, a weakling who would be scared of a girl like Birdie. No one ever saw Buck with a girl. He stayed close at home with his aging father, Henley Humphries, and was seldom out after night.

A picture of Birdie came to Luster now: her eyes black as chimney soot, her brownish skin giving a passionlike beauty to her. She sure had taken the boys in. She always had a string of them after her, which made it harder to name Buck Humphries.

Luster took the road to Brother Lazenby's house. The minister had been at Firbank ten years. He preached at the Nazarene church-house, Sobby, which overlooked the Nation country from one of the highest West Neeley hills. Luster had never heard him preach. Indirectly Brother Lazenby had tried to get Luster to bring Dossie Bell out of the hills and marry her. He said God would be angry until he did. The minister sent women of the church to Luster's cabin to give the warning. They had come while Luster was known to be away. Brother Lazenby himself had been. He took a great interest in Dossie Bell. He said he wasn't forgetting she was a soul to save. Luster paid them no heed.

It didn't make much difference now whether Brother Lazenby came to his cabin. She was dead and it didn't matter any longer. But he supposed it was the best thing to do in death. She would want a preacher even if it was the one who led in her churching. He never understood Brother Lazenby's great power over Dossie Bell. The preacher knew what to do in sickness and he'd helped lay-out many a corpse. Dossie Bell had gone to church often to hear him preach. She would want him to put her away. He was necessary in death.

Sudie, the minister's wife, answered Luster's "Hello." She held a coaloil-lamp up toward his face and peered at him over gold-rimmed glasses. Luster had seen Sudie Lazenby few times before. She was just entering middle-age and her eyes were a sort of wideopen yellow-green; searching, restless eyes. Luster thought them pretty, sadly, meekly, so. Her nose was a little long. He liked her mouth: it looked soft and warm and kind of clinginglike.

"Who is it?" she asked, lowering the lamp to gaze beyond its beams. A rising lip of flame touched the chimney with a smudge of soot.

Luster wasn't sure what to say. He had expected to see the preacher. His jumper and overalls were dust-caked. His hair, in the lamplight, was sweatstreaked with brown trash particles. He looked at the tall thin woman, scarcely aware he had ever seen her before. Sudie Lazenby was town-folks. She'd been raised in Arkansas. Luster didn't know how to talk to a woman of her type. He had never cared to and the occasion had never before presented itself. He reckoned she would understand death.

"Hit's Luster Holder, Miss Lazenby. I want to see Brother Lazenby. My woman's dead."

Her eyes widened in wonder. She stared at the tall hillman, fascinated. Stories crossed her mind: Holder, Luster Holder: it had always been the name, a name suggestive of something dire, damning. It was hard for her to believe she was face to face with him. She tried to think herself afraid of one who had caused so much county gossip, whose forefathers had wrested the western end of Neeley from the Tobly outlaws, little caring that they had to shed blood to do so; the man who had taken a woman to live with him without God's sanction.

"Dossie Bell dead?" she found herself saying. "I do declare!" She paused, uncertain, silhouetted in the doorway. "I guess you better come in, Mr. Holder, and tell me all about it. I do say it!" It was hard to hide her uneasiness in the presence of this man. Her desire for news overcame her timidity. She talked on as she led him into the parlor. She talked like a woman who was starved for company, conversation.

"Brother Lazenby ain't in right now. He's over to the schoolhouse. Professor Barker is giving a box-supper to buy new desks. And you know how they need them. The children have been setting on planks all the year. Dossie Bell dead? Ain't it awful? She was such a purty woman. I'm nearly crazy to know how it happened. Set down, Mr. Holder."

"I dunno, Miss Lazenby. I dunno. I come in and thar she lay on the bed stiff and cole." He spoke sulkingly, like a little boy being pumped for news.

The chair was soft. He entered a half doze. Sudie looked at him questioningly, as if she were afraid he would fall asleep here in the room with her.

"You must be tired, Mr. Holder. I'll get you some sassafras tea. No trouble at all. I'm keeping some hot for the minister. Make yourself at home while I'm gone."

With his foot Luster shoved away a red carpet-covered footstool. Limply one elbow hung over an arm of his chair. His wrist dangled into a magazine rack which was half filled with carefully stacked religious periodicals: Nazarene, Methodist, Campbellite, Baptist, Primitive Baptist, Pentecostal; and the Yellow Jacket.

Luster rested his other hand on a small cross-grained table under a smoking parlor lamp. The red-bellied china shade of the lamp threw a silver circle upon the polished red cherry. The light attracted insects.

The sleepy hillman watched them: every shape, size and color.

Most of them were jumpers: little oblong things as big as a match-head: tomato-red and ocher; raspberry purple and faint pale blue. The jumpers were blunt and jerky; they flipped suddenly into the light and snapped abruptly out. There were flies with filmy wings: jade webbed with gold; translucent ungovernable wings as large as Luster's thumbnail. These flies had jointed rodlike bodies. There were moths and beetles.

The circle of light was in constant action. The insects crawled, swooped, clicked, fluttered, glided, flopped into vision and out. They cut about the lamp in parabolas and zigzags, weaving an eternal pattern.

A brown fur-crested junebug struck the table with a sharp *crack*. He lighted on his back and righted himself by waving long fingerlike legs in the air. He looked at Luster with his vicious luminous ruby eyes and, after several unsuccessful attempts, whirred his crisp wings into action and left the light in a half-spiral, half-curlicue. A moment later Luster heard him butt his head against the ceiling.

There were tiny delicate moths: rose and tan; coral and lavender. Tiger moths with black-and-yellow striped underwings. Flimsy silver ladylike moths as metallic as milkweed down.

All in movement. All in chaotic movement.

Mrs. Lazenby came in with the tea. Luster took a cup. It was steaming and smelled good. Sudie sat down and began talking. Luster liked to watch her warm-looking mouth as the words came out. He could almost see the words crawl from her tongue. Through the slits of his drooping lids his eyes stayed resolutely upon her. She kept her own moving to and from him as she talked. She talked as if she wanted never to stop; never to let silence fall between them, to be alone with this man and silence.

"It's sure too bad about Dossie Bell. It's a sight of trouble has come into the country this past season. Shelby Haines had a gentleman-cow struck by lightning last Tuesday night. He left it out in the pasture. Of course the meat wasn't no good after he found it." She stopped. "And—" She stopped short, her face crimsoning; then plunged on in a wavering voice. "Have you heard about Square Kiler's daughter, Birdie?"

"No, I hain't that I recollec', Miss Lazenby," Luster mumbled, half-asleep.

("I've got to speak on it," she though uneasily. "I begun and now I've got to talk on a subject to a man to which it shouldn't be talked.")

"Well," she began unsteadily, "she—she's run around with the boys a lot lately. The good Lord knows she's too young for that, not being but eighteen and all. She went out with Buck Humphries last spring and he completely disgraced her. It was other side of the Refuge church in the Neylor settlement. She told her father a night or two ago. Buck ain't been seen since."

Luster caught his eyelids. They were almost closed.

"He orght to haft to marry her," he mumbled.

She warmed to her subject, forgetting her embarrassment. It was as if she were charging the rights of all women to this man.

"He ought to be lynched. Ruining a nice girl like Birdie! We've got to uphold innocent womankind. The Square's het up. It ain't going to do Buck any good when him or her Uncle Luke Tolby either one finds him."

Luster forced himself to rise from the comfortable chair. He looked at Sudie Lazenby through hooded eyes.

"I got to be goin', Miss Lazenby. I got to see kin I find the preacher. I 'low he kin be a help now. I'll drop by the box-supper."

"Do by all means, Mr. Holder. It looks like there's goin' to be weather. The sky's smoothed over. I think it's just too awful about Dossie Bell. I'll try to get over for the setting up sometime tonight. I guess the funeral'll be up to Sobby tomorrow?"

"I hain't shore, Miss Lazenby."

She didn't accompany him to the front door.

The damp freshness of the night air made Luster wide awake. It was getting late.

He took the road to the Firbank schoolhouse. It was lighter now. Thin gray clouds veiled the face of the moon. Dust pressed up over his shoes; his sockless feet slipped back and forth on the leather like it was velvet he was treading on. If it didn't rain soon, everything would burn to a crisp.

Everybody was worked up over Buck and Birdie. It was being talked and made worse all the time. Squire Heber Kiler's girl, Birdie, was well known. Old women of Firbank had said she was weeding a wide row. This very thing was bound to happen. She'd started out young and taken her raising into her own hands. Millie Kiler, her mommey, had tried to raise her right. She'd worked out her life for the Squire and Birdie. Folks were just glad of something new and dirty to talk about.

Luster recalled how Birdie had stopped him once on the Meedon Levee road. He mended her bridle while she talked boisterously, laughing laughs which drummed hard against the wall of cypress. He said little to her. She was pretty as the very mischief until she talked.

"She just throwed her purtiness away in rough talk like I never keered for a woman to talk. I didn't give a whoop about her. She was just like a young rooster which comb is gittin' red. Hit tard the hell outen me even to listen to her. If she'd a-kept her mouth shut and hadn't bin so loud, hit might of bin different. I cain't believe a puny little feller like Buck Humphries ever done anything to her. She'd skeer the paste outen him."

Thoughts of Buck clouded his mind. "I couldn't never git hit straight why Dossie Bell seemed to keer so much for Buck. He come over to the cabin when I wasn't there and helped her with the work. He's hung round her every sinst he was a little shaver. She always took up for him when other folks rode him. She's the only one he'd ever talk to. She must-a pitied him and sorter mothered him. He never knowed his mommey and no one else did. They say Henley Humphries hain't his pappy. He takened him in because he was sorry for orphants. It hain't for me to know. Old Henley he talked religion to him till the boy's afeered to say peas. He acts skeered of me. He takes out in a hurry the minute he sees me. Hell far, I wouldn't tech a hair on his head, though just seein' him so weak and fraidy-like and all is enough to pesticate any feller.

"He talks to Dossie Bell or sets lookin' off some'rs or nother like he was outen his skin and up in the cloud-banks. Nobody likes Buck 'cause he's strange. They hate his old pappy. I hain't got nothin' a-tall agin neither of them. And not no time much for them.

"I 'low Dossie Bell would be bad worried if she knowed he was in trouble. Buck may have did hit, but I hain't keerin' none."

3

THERE WERE A HUNDRED or more people at the Firbank schoolhouse.

Wagons and buggies with a small scattering of cars covered the hilly grounds. The house was full. People were sitting in the windows. Outside, near the front door, some men and boys were passing a Mason-jar of whisky among them, laughing, slapping backs, and scuffling. One boy, drunker than the others, kept singing low and mournfully:

"Thought I heerd somebody shout,
Tater-bug, tater-bug, takin' out."

Luster stopped near the open doorway.

He could hear Doddler Horn, Firbank school board president, auctioning off the boxes. Dodler was said to be the best auctioneer in all Neeley County. He was an ex-superintendent of Public Instruction. He had never finished the eigth grade, but there wasn't a word in the Old Blue Back Speller he couldn't spell. He had taught for years and was the only man in the county to hold a first-class life certificate— one which enabled him to teach any subject. He had obtained it from the State Superintendent, who was a friend. He had gone all the way to Nashville to get it.

Doddler was holding up the boxes one by one. A price would be quoted, quickly followed by shouts and laughter. Quiet again and a raised figure. More laughter and talk, giggling and whistling and stamping of feet.

"Come on, folks!" Doddler shouted in a squeaking voice. "Come on and get this here!" He fidgeted with the crepe-paper on the box in his hand. "Our women-folks has walked their hind legs off gettin' all sorta good things cooked up. Wonder what's in this here? I wish I knew. I'll bet they ain't no cholera hen in it. No, sirree. No, sir." He grinned a mouthful of battered gold teeth at the crowd and winked. "I heard it hinted out that there's some good chittlings in somebody's box rolled in flour and fried brown. I'm here to tell you I could eat a chittling long as from here to Trotter's Landin' on the Tennessee River. I sometimes wish they wouldn't cut them up a-tall. Come on, folks, git them dollars out of your jeans. We got to git some desks bought for our little fellers."

Luster knew what was happening. They were raising the boxes on the fellows who were in love. He walked up the steps and stopped in the schoolhouse door. The sputtering gaslights were a blinding white. He looked over the crowd before him. His burning eyes saw a mixture of ruffles, white collars, black stockings.

People stared at him. They all knew Luster Holder. They knew he seldom came out of his part of the hills. He and his woman lived an isolated life back there. If he came out, it meant something was wrong.

Luster stepped back out of the light. He didn't want to mix with the crowd, the curious faces. He leaned against the doorjamb and watched, casual, disinterested.

The auctioneering had ceased. Little Lurline Sipes was reciting:

"God love the little children,
And their fathers and mothers too,
We live to make folks happy;
Spreading sunshine for you."

She sat down and tucked her dress about her thighs. There were handclaps, whistling, stamping, intermingled with shrilling laughter.

Luster saw Brother Lazenby. The minister was making an announcement.

Brother Lazenby was tall and thin. He held his hands behind him as he talked. His eyes were like small black berries. His brown hair, which grew far back to expose his wisdom peaks, was beginning to show his scalp in several places. As he talked, he emphasized each word by smacking his mouth so tightly shut that it left his face in the midst of an expression of half-grin and half-frown. Tonight he was obviously ill at ease. He kept glancing from side to side as he talked.

After his announcement he stepped out at a side door and began fanning with a handkerchief. Luster walked around the corner of the house and went up to him. He was a full head taller than the minister.

"Brother Lazenby, I want you to come to my cabin with me."

The minister started. He looked at Luster suspiciously.

"I'm afraid I don't know you, my good man." He recognized Luster. Through all his years in Firbank, he had heard of Luster Holder. This was his first meeting with the hillman. Luster had been pointed out to him in Melburg one Saturday. Brother Lazenby had been to plead with Dossie Bell to forsake her sinful life, but had picked times when Luster was away from the cabin.

As he looked at the tall brown man, worrying thoughts flashed through his mind—of Dossie Bell's churching, of his sermons against her and this calm man, of his last visit to Luster's cabin. What could the big hillman want with him? He was seized with a grave uneasiness. Had she exposed him?

Luster put a finger to the side of his nose and blew hard out into the night.

"I'm Luster Holder. You recollec' me?"

"Sure. Sure," Brother Lazenby said unsteadily, clearing his throat over and over. "Yes, Brother Holder, I call you to mind."

"Dossie Bell, my woman, is dead."

Brother Lazenby looked up dully, his mouth sagging. A fleeting picture of the cabin flashed across his brain: the cabin in the pines with Dossie Bell there cold in death: Dossie Bell the woman whose soul he had tried to save.

He swallowed hard and fought off a sickness which rose in the pit of his stomach. When he spoke, his voice was more hollow and mechanical; and now, underneath the tones of it was a real, a growing fear.

"Dossie Bell's gone away," he said stupidly. He seemed trying to convince himself of what he knew to be true. Then to Luster, falteringly, "I give you my best sympathy, Brother Holder. The Black Angel of Death comes when we ain't looking for it. We can't see nor know why our dear ones are taken. The Lord, Our Father, always knows best."

"I 'lowed as you was a preacher, you'd know what to do. Dossie Bell is still in the cabin. I figger she'd want a preacher in the house."

Brother Lazenby held his hands behind his back. "I mustn't let on I don't want to go," he thought. "I got to fight this thing out down to scratch. I can't give up. I got to keep a hold on myself."

The fact that Luster had come to him for advice made him feel better. His services were needed. In death he was the one whom they called. But now he couldn't go. He couldn't return to the cabin. A shudder ran over his thin body.

"Something must be done, Brother Holder," he said in fagged tones. "The ways of Providence are unscrutable, but we know He doeth all things well." He probed his mind for an excuse which would release him.

"Come on over there and maybe you kin tell more," Luster said drowsily.

"Sure. Sure." He paused. "As yet, Brother Holder, you can't realize your loss. It will be days before the Angel of Mercy heals your heart." He paused again and rubbed his palms together. "I tried to keep Dossie Bell in the folds of the church. I fear she will be questioned before the Final Judge."

His lips quivered as he awaited the effects of his words, words he had forced from his mouth in a stall for time.

Impatiently Luster shifted his feet.

"She was a good woman. I 'low she'll git in if anybody does."

Again Brother Lazenby forced his words, preparatory to building an argument which would keep him from having to go with the hillman.

"The Lord remembers," he said slowly. "If you'll only give your hand and heart to Jesus Lord, the Only Begotten Son of the Holy Ghost, you can enter the Joy which passeth all understanding and be reunited with Dossie Bell." It was hard to tell what to say to this man. Luster had kept Dossie Bell from being a Christian. He was directly responsible to God for her lost soul.

Something in the way the hillman stood, slouched, unconcerned, dismayed the minister. He knew he must rid himself of this man before it was too late. He couldn't stand it away out there alone with Luster and death.

Luster was very much whipped down. He had made a wide circle to find the preacher. He had left his cabin, cut around the edge of the Nation, and walked along the ridge to the schoolhouse. He was anxious to get back where he could rest.

Brother Lazenby's words fell meaninglessly on his ears.

"I'm terribly sorry, but I can't go with you, Brother Holder," the preacher was saying in a pleading voice. "Not tonight. I'm tired out and Sudie is alone. We'll come over at daybreak. You'll have to get somebody else. I figure Henley Humphries will go. He'll know just how to take ahold."

Luster grasped one of Lazenby's frail arms.

'We'uns'ull hafta hurry if we beat the rain," he said in a dead voice.

Further words stuck in the minister's throat. He walked to his buggy. Luster's eyes were trying to close. He climbed into the seat and slowly they drove from the school grounds.

Rain was threatening again: the moon was whitely blurred in the solid gray gauze of the sky.

4

JUST AT DUSK-DARK Wurner came into Urfie Pearl
Buckner's yard where she sat with Clemmie Bean.
When Urfie Pearl saw the short thick-set man making
route to her house, she said, "Our Lord proteck us,
Clemmie. It's Wurner Crouse. We're in for a set."

Everybody in the Nation country knew Wurner
Crouse. His pappy said the boy—the nam now: he
was forty or more years old—had been born with
turtle eggs instead of brains, that his mommey got
scared at a turtle while she was heavy with him. He
was marked. Folks said he had a strong back and a
weak mind. He was built like a stud horse: stubby,
stocky: so short, according to Luke Tolby, that he
couldn't sneeze without getting sand in his eyebrows.
The harder the work, the better he liked it. He could
work all morning clearing newground, digging

stumps, tearing poison-ivy from tree-trunks with his bare hands; and then spend the afternoon grabbing for fish under logs or in holes of the river-bank. It was claimed he could strip barbed-wire barehanded or twist the short horns off a bull.

He was very religious and never missed church. He sat on the front bench and sang louder than anyone, his voice a resounding bass. He visited back and forth over the Nation. He would drop in at mealtime and stay a week or more if he took a mind. He gave people a good settin' at any time and argued loud and long on Scripture. He emphasized each point by slapping a stubby hand flat against the floor or wall and saying, "What do you'uns think of that?"

He held a doglike affection for Luster and Dossie Bell. Luster had been good to him and seen that no one imposed on him. Once Luster had dropped by a party and found several fellows plaguing Wurner. The big hillman remember John Holder's words, "Don't pick on no idiot nor hit no cripple." He had cleaned out the house: men had flown out of there like blackbirds from a wheatfield.

Wurner kept his friends warned of danger and posted on the latest happenings. Outside of Urfie Peal Buckner he was the best newscarrier in the Nation. He would come down the road, kicking up dust, singing religious hymns, and shooting railroad taps, which he gathered in Melburg on Saturdays, from his slingshot at posts and trees or anything he took a mind to shoot.

People remembered how he had been knocked down by an automobile at Firbank. One report said, "He got up dustin' hissef off, smilin' like a cat eatin' paste and shoutin', 'Hain't hurt me none yit as the little boy says!'"

He inherited a strip of land from an uncle. The county court had to take it over and watch after it for him when he swapped it to a negro for a Barlow knife.

"It shore is Wurner now," Urfie Pearl repeated. "I pray he's just passin' some news round. I shore-God hope he ain't wantin' to eat. He's most generally always so hungry he can eat a body out of house and home and then start in on the barn roof."

Wurner approached them in a queer waddling walk. A slim-legged brown cur moved out stiffly to meet him, growling, the short hair ruffling on the rising rolls of skin at its neck. Wurner drew out his slingshot and aimed it, his little eyes twinkling. "I shoot you now. I mean I shoot you fastly now."

"Come on back here, Chaphard," Urfie called. "He's gittin' so lordly mean, Clemmie, we cain't do nothin' with him sinst Harve started feedin' him gunpowder. But Harve has bin missin' meat from the smokehouse. He hast to keep the dog edged."

"I'd lock him up now, Urfie, while it's about to storm. You durn well know dogs draws lighnin'."

Chaphard backed under the house.

Wurner spraddled out on the ground at their feet. The two old women waited impatiently for him to say something, Urfie Pearl's palsied head aquiver, her hand to one ear anxious to hear.

"She's dead, as the feller says, dead all right, all right," Wurner said hoarsely, glumly. Tobacco juice drooled from the corners of his wide mouth.

"Who's dead?" the two women asked together.

"I went up there. I went up there now and went in there. She wouldn't git up nor move none. Luster was off. He was off and she's dead now."

"Is it Dossie Bell?" Urfie asked eagerly. She leaned forward in her chair.

"Dossie Bell's gone way off. Luster hain't there now." He fingered his slingshot in short heavy hands. He pushed to his feet. "I'm goin' on. I'm tellin' ever'body she's dead all right." He waddled from the yard and on down the hill path to the big-road.

Dark came on suddenly while the old women tilted against the house wall in their creaky chairs. They talked the startling news, making plans to go over for the sitting-up.

They dipped from their snuffboxes: the sound of lids being pulled off; the sharp spitting onto packed ground. They studied the weather, trying to decide if the end of the drouth was near; trying to decide if they could make it to Luster's cabin before the rain.

"The lightnin' keeps twinkerin' here and yon, Urfie. It may come on us yit," Clemmie ventured.

Urfie Pearl sucked in her snuff. "That heavy cloud looks like a weather breeder. The prayin' over to Sobby may of hope, Clemmie."

"I'm a-doubtin' it. Folks is entirely too wicked now. The Lord's a-metin' out his punishment. Brother Lazenby was bin a warnin' of them." Clemmie talked over her toothbrush.

Urfie Pearl seemed in deep study before she spoke, as if she were collecting each word and placing it in rigid order.

"Clemmie, I ain't never spoke out my mind on this here and I wouldn't keer for it to git no further. Ardie Percy she named it to me and swore me up not to tell. But knowin' you kin keep shut-mouth on nigh anything, I'm gonna tell you."

Clemmie stopped chewing her brush.

"I'm on far coals to be a-knowin'."

"Ardie she tole me over to the Refuge church squirrel-stew. She said her man was cuttin' through Luster's south woods one day last week on his way to Firbank. He seen someone hid in the willows a-watchin' Luster's cabin. He hid hissef behind a scaly-bark tree and waited. He seen Luster leave the cabin and figgered he was goin' down to the still.

"Well, sir, after Luster left, the feller behind the willows creeped out, half bent over, and run lickety-split across the paster and went through the kitchen door."

"For God's sake, who was it?"

"Brother Winnie Lazenby hissef!"

"May my heart skip a beat!"

"It's the cold-curdled truth, Clemmie. Ardie Percy nor her man neither don't lie."

"What do you figger?"

"I hate to think. When I tole Miz Murkison and Luler Winkle about it out to Murdie Cote's quiltin' last first Monday, they hooted at the idear. They're shore wropped up in that preacher."

"Brother Lazenby's mouth ain't no prayer book even if it does open and shut. I've always said that. Sudie shore orght to know about it."

"She wouldn't say nothin'. She's afeered of her man. She cain't rule him no more than she kin fly to Glory. I hear tell her and the preacher sleeps in sep'rate rooms. I never knowed the like. I've suscpicioned a lot about that minister since I seen he was agin turnin' Dossie Bell out at Sobby."

"She shore takened him in. Wait'll he's found out some day. He'll crawl in a hole and drag it in after him, if Luster Holder don't knife him first."

"Dossie Bell always was the kind of a hussy which set the men to prancin'. Her pertendin' to love the church! I was in favor of startin' up a bunch and runnin' her outen the county. But you couldn't git no man to help. And I'm ready to gracefully admit nothin' couldn't be did as long as she was hangin' out with Luster Holder. I wonder does he know wood's bein' stole offen his land? My man says it shore is bein' took, but he wasn't gonna say nothin' to Luster. He don't want to git messed up with him."

"There'll be some more killin's if Luster hears. There's enough devilment goin' on. His woman's death's a judgment sent agin him."

"Her and Birdie Kiler's two of a kind. You've heerd about Birdie?"

"I wasn't surprised one mite. I knowed she'd git a teat caught in the fence the way she was bollyfox-in' around."

"She flies about Firbank not wearin' enough clothes to flag no handcar if they was all red. And her all swole up like a cow foundered on green peas!"

"That ole Square's to blame. He's raised her like she was a slut-dog stid of a human. He treats Millie worse'n he does them nigger wenches on his bottom farm. The pore thing won't be here long. That white-swellin' and heart misery's gonna jerk here out 'fore grapes git ripe agin."

"I hate the sin outen that ole Square. I'd like to hit him 'tween the eyes with a set of buzzard guts."

"It's the Lord God truth!"

"He's always laughin' in yore face, openin' up that hairy ole mouth of his'n with a low-flunged joke. His mouth puts me in the mind of a closed bird's nest which opens and shows a settin' of rotten eggs inside."

"Yeh, and his breath smells like fresh-corded wood. I wouldn't trust him no further'n you kin throw a mule by the tail."

"Lord naw, I wouldn't risk him in a manure pile with a muzzle on."

Urfie looked up at the gathering clouds. "We could go out there but this here threatin' weather's got me hangin' 'tween a chill and a sweat."

"We better be waitin' a while. It's bound to do something soon one way or nother. They'll be needin' help."

"I know, Clemmie, but Luster he ain't beholdin' to nobody. You cain't tell how he'll take it."

"That's true as truth. But I ain't gonna miss it."

Urfie Pearl cleared her throat. "Did you know they ain't nothin' so bad after corpses as cats?" Her voice was low, confidential.

"That's what they say, Urfie. They's evil in them. They know when a body's gonna die."

"They'll git in and set right on the corpse's chist and eat its face."

"I mind," Clemmie said haltingly, "when my man was throwed on his back with flux. It was about last tater-diggin' time. I needed money to buy me some liver regulator, oil and other medicines. I went to Spivey Hale over to Melburg. He's forgot how he come from out here up from nothin'. Feels like a millionaire now he's cashierin' at the bank. He made he didn't know me and wouldn't let me have a cent. It flew all over me."

"Did you put him in his place?"

"I'm comin' to that. There was several strangers in the bank, so I fared both barrels at him. I says, 'I mind the time when yore old pappy pertendin' to practice medicine out to Firbank. His ole hoss was so pore a puff of wind would of blowed it outen the county. He used ole strings and plowlines for harness.' I says, "I set up when yore sister was a corpse.

It was the downright nastiest house I ever seen. It kept one busy drivin' away the mangiest cats ever borned while the other two of us picked chinch-bugs off the corpse to keep it from bein' eat up.' I shore laid him out."

"You heerd his lesson right down to scratch. Clemmie, I think I'll git Harve to take Spiddy and her six kitten down where we'uns won't see her hair nor hide of them agin."

"Wy, cheese and crackers! I ain't go not use for cats no way, form, nor fashion." She paused and listened. "Who's that comin', Urfie?"

They both listened, their chairs flat on the ground.

"Hello, Urfie Pearl! Hello!" The voice low, guttural.

"It's Granny Blackburn, Clemmie. She's heerd of Dossie Bell. Come on up, Granny!"

"You better come out and hep me, Urfie. My laigs are fizzled. I cain't git over the last ridge here."

Urfie and Clemmie felt their way down the ridge where the old woman stood bent over on a stick. One on each side they helped her back to the house and eased her into a chair.

Granny Blackburn breathed out in a sigh. "I swar to God that 'ere walk's hamstrung me. I feel like I'd bin drug through hell back'ards and beat to death with a soot bag. I guess you'uns has heerd of Dossie dyin'. I was on my way there, but my laigs has tuck out. I'll haft to stop here and rest up a while anyhow."

"You shouldn't of tried to git over there by yor-eself, Granny," Clemmie said.

"I'll git thar or die dead tryin'," the old woman retorted angrily.

Clemmie and Urfie were silent. Then Urfie said, yawning, "I guess we kin all settle here and see what the weather's gonna do. My man kin hitch up and haul us over in the waggin. How'd you hear about Dossie Bell?"

"Of course, you know we'uns is on a party line," Granny began. "I cain't git round like I uster so I keep the phone for news. Hit's expensive, but I cain't do without hit. My darter, Norey, she kivers the box most of the day, my hearin' not bein' good as hit wonst was. But I take my turn. About a hour ago she was settin' thar with the ear-piece to her ear a-prayin' some'un would talk. Her prayers was answered. Thar was three longs and a short. Sudie Lazenby was cal-lin' Elmer Runnels askin' him if he'd drive her over to Holder's. Luster had bin thar. His woman had quit on him right short off. I 'low the news is knowrated by now. Ever'body that had phones was on them. Hit made listenin' hard."

"Well, I do say it! We was just talkin' on how hard it is to keep cats out where there's dead folks at."

Granny Blackburn spat and cackled, her spirits rising.

"I guess I've sot up nigh a hundred times," she said hoarsely, taking in her breath wheezingly. "Every sinst I was a young gal I never miss no settin'-ups.

I've hepped lay out a-many a corpse. Now I have. Hit jest seems to come nateral with me. When a body dies any whar's nigh me, they say, 'Send fer Mertie Blackburn,' and I comes a-humpin' hit.

"I disremember jest how long hit's been, but hit was at the settin-up over Meander Mercer, Banford Mercer's idiot gal. We'uns had bin argufyin' right sprightly on how the soul gits outen the house when a body dies. Some said if the winders was down, hit clumb the chimley hole. But I figgered that was why the cats come. They was atter the soul.

"Ever'body had went off to bed and left hit to me. I'd jest went in to wet the camphor rag on Meander's face. I raised the edge of the sheet which kivered her, and what do you'uns suppose I seed? Meander's big ole gray-green tomcat, Harmy Topsy Don, a-settin' on her chist eatin' on her face. Hit had already et away one whole side and was gittin' set fer t'other."

The other women listened attentively, much interested.

"What did you do when you seen the cat?" asked Urfie Pearl.

Granny Blackburn cackled. "I jest sorter shooed hit offen her and says, 'Go rest yoresef and let Meander's soul be.'"

"So I jest tole Norey this evenin' while she set a-washin' hippens fer the baby. I jest tole Norey when I heerd Dossie Bell had thumped out. I jest tole Norey, 'I'm a-goin' over and hep keep nothin'

from botheratin' her.' Norey she says, 'That's gonna
be weather, Mommey. Hit's gonna storm godawful.
I'd be afeered.' But I says, 'The Lord nor nobody else
hain't never concocked no storm that'll hole me off
when thar's a corpse to be seed atter.'"

"There may not be no storm," Clemmie said,
looking skyward. " 'Pears like it's about to break off."

5

A THICK CLOUD deepened and blackened across the forest-covered west. Big gray-steel drops of rain hit scatteringly into the dust before Luster's cabin and sent tiny smokelike circles into the cooling air.

The darkish cedars rocked as the wind hissed through them; grass and weeds blew low and lay flat against the dry cracked ground, to rise up again as the gusts lessened. The chain and weight which kept the palinged-gate closed rattled and squeaked hoarsely. Packer and Hobart growled and ran under the house.

The rain came harder.

The drought was breaking up. Water spanked the rust-eaten tin roof with a steady hum and rolled to the ground in a spatter of gray and brown.

Within the cabin all was soot black: dark from the hole of the chimney opening on back beyond the low bed in the corner and up to the obscureness of the smokened rafters; dark and blotted out except when washed now and again by the lightning fire.

In the big-room Dossie Bell lay across the bed, cold in death. The tall mantel clock ticked hoarsely, dully, vacantly, bearing down on the room almost noisily.

Against the roof the now-increasing drops sheeted themselves into a clanking roar. Wind circled the corners of the cabin, flapped its loose whitewashed planks, shook it on its woodblock pillars, sent the kitchen door banging back and forth on its weak rusty hinges. Sharp thunderclaps cracked here and yonder, growling away in the black denseness toward Melburg.

Balky was lowing loudly, more distressed from neglect. Cooter and Carnes, the gray mules, stampeded about their lot, kicking high, whinnying out into the electrified air.

In the heat of darkness Dossie Bell lay cold, dead and alone.

From behind the latticed-in henhouse came the first of the dismal sounds: a wail. It rose high and faded far away against the blackened hillsides; grew nearer and fell onto the roof of Luster's cabin; seeped down into the burrowed darkness of the chimney. It was answered from the peach-orchard, from the springhouse down in the sheep-pasture, from the tall sedgebrush on the road-banks. The cries mingled piercingly and settled together agonizingly until in one weirdly-wrought chorus they centered on the big-room where the hill-woman lay dead.

The cats had scented death. On the soft cushions of their feet they stalked the cabin.

The rain burst from the blackish sky in flooding furry; the hot-and-cold August wind lifted dust and leaves and sticks to mix and mingle with the continuous downpour.

The cats stalked the house.

From the big-room their fine detecting noses felt out the corpse. On the tail of each flurry of wind came the scent of the stiffening body.

The clock, its face now dim except when the sky split open in a moment of silvered fire, said eleven. Each flash cut out the dimmest features of the room: the four-poster bed; Dossie Bell's white drawn face; the chair by the window. Against the screens, steel-gripping claws set fiercely, scraped desperately. At the door to the big-room came the grating of more claws, the mournful whines which ended in the same agonizing wails.

The screen on the south window was loose. It shook and gave at the lower left-hand corner. A dark paw tore it away, a tawny head appeared. A lithe, sleek black body vaulted to the floor and sent two gold-yellow prying lights searching about the deathroom.

Silent, cold, the hill-woman stretched across the bed. Her thin body pushed, melted, far down into the large choky featherbed. One of her slippers was untied. A nickel-sized hole in a black cotton stocking exposed the white of one of her legs. Her gray-checked gingham dress was pulled tight, folded and twisted beneath her knees as she had fallen. Two more cats found the torn screen and leaped through to the cabin floor. They approached the bed.

The rain increased; the storm broke with renewed fierceness. Thunder ran across the sky and rumbled off into the distance like someone driving a log-wagon over a hardened clay road.

A horse neighed loudly. A buggy rattled. Packer and Hobart barked sharply and rushed through the sheet of water to greet their master. Brother Lazenby and Luster, water-soaked, shivering and uncomfortable in the cooling atmosphere, had reached the cabin.

6

LUSTER HELD Brother Lazenby's old mare while the preacher climbed from the buggy. The lightning revealed their water-soaked condition. The minister's thin seersucker suit clung to his skinny limbs, stuck to him in tightening wrinkles. The coat was lumpy at the shoulders. Drops of water rolled from the brim of his black felt hat and worked slowly down his forehead and cheeks like beads of grease. He kept drawing a hand across his wet brow.

Luster's shirt was a darker blue. His jumper was stiff and clung in hardened, ropelike folds.

He led the preacher into the room where his woman lay a corpse. The minister stayed close to the hillman. In the darkness Luster could feel Brother Lazenby's shaking body. He found a match and lighted a lamp.

The dim gleam struck yellowy over their sodden forms. Gingerly, Brother Lazenby let his eyes pass from Luster's drawn face and rest flinching on the still figure on the bed.

Dossie Bell looked cold and dry. Luster came to the foot of the bed. Silently the two of them, Luster and the minister, stood watching the dead woman.

Luster's face was solemn. He raised his eyes to the preacher. Brother Lazenby's expression of horror caused the big hillman to start back from the bed, to turn almost mechanically to where a Marlin 30-30 hung on a rack above the door leading into the hallway.

With a quaking hand Brother Lazenby pointed to Dossie Bell. Seated on the dead woman's chest was a small gray cat. So perfectly did it blend into the gray checks of Dossie Bell's dress that it had been indiscernible to Luster's tired stinging eyes.

The cat had not touched the corpse. It sat purring gently, its glassy yellow eyes intent on Dossie Bell's waxy face.

Luster walked quickly forward. With a hollow moan, the cat vaulted from the hill-woman's chest and disappeared through the hole in the screen. Almost instantly, three other cats came from beneath the bed and followed in the wake of their retreating leader.

Wails and moans arose from out of the soggy dark. Brother Lazenby walked to the rocking-chair and sat down.

Luster said, "I just come in and there she lay cold and dead."

Brother Lazenby made no answer. He was listening to the moans outside the house. They continued low, now close; then far away. Claws again grated across the screens.

The rain was holding up. They could hear it clicking through the heavy cedars in front of the cabin.

Luster moved toward the door. "You wait here. I got to go and fasten up them chickens. The cats'll git in and riddle them shore. Dossie Bell never neglected them before. Minks and weasels is bad too."

Brother Lazenby got up from the chair. He still had on his hat, its brim dripping with water.

"I'll go with you, Brother Holder. I can't stay in here alone." The minister spoke more naturally now.

"I won't be a minute, Brother Lazenby. You'll get wet agin. Dossie Bell shore wants her hens barred up from them cats."

"I know, Brother Holder. I know. I'll go with you."

Luster was gone before the preacher could follow him. He stepped under the clothesline. One of Dossie Bell's brown-domestic underskirts hung from the line: drawn-up and dripping with water. The peach-tree leaves glistened, for the clouds had parted, the moon showing dull, yellow-white, like a cracked marble, through the rift. The rent in the sky was closing. More rain was bound to come.

The wet jumper and trousers clung unpleasantly to Luster's chilled limbs. He rolled up his pants and slid his heavy brogans over weeds and grass. The chickens cackled as he barred the henhouse door. He threw a half-brick at Tommyjohn, Dossie Bell's cat. It scurried away toward the barn. The hounddogs bounced from beneath the cabin and ran howling after Tommyjohn and the other cats.

Tommyjohn was Dossie Bell's cat, but she'd tried to eat her face. Luster had liked the cat. Now he had no more use for it. Dossie Bell had picked it up on the Meedon Levee road the other side of the river. It was half-starved, its ribs like warped staves. She brought it for miles. She fed it and made a bed for it in the woodbox behind the kitchen stove.

Stolidly the big hillman thought of it:

"You went out nights and got full of kitten and Dossie Bell she taken keer of you. When you showed up carryin' one, with six followin' you, she bedded you'uns out under the crib.

"But what do you do, Tommyjohn? Soon as she dies on me, soon as she cain't tote no more pitchers of sweetmilk to yore's and yorn, you clumb the screen. You tore hit out at the bottom. You sneaked in and jumped on her chist and would of ate into her face if I hadn't come."

He had thought that it was the right thing for Dossie Bell to have Brother Lazenby come to the cabin. The preacher hadn't wanted to come. He had pestered Dossie Bell with his church doings while she lived. But now that she was dead, he didn't want to see her. He was afraid of death.

"I cain't see why a man'ud be skeered of anything dead. Hit's the livin' you hafta watch. I'll hafta go back in there with him or he'll take out for home."

Brother Lazenby was left in the big-room with Dossie Bell. He had been in the presence of death before, but others were near him. He hadn't been out alone in the Nation's hills with a man like Luster and in the same room with the woman he knew he had betrayed. Luster had forced him to come to the cabin. Now, he was not sure what to do, how to ever get away and back home.

He had heard the legend of cats in death. Tonight with his own eyes he had seen the cat on the corpse: Dossie Bell's cat, Tommyjohn, sitting on her chest, fixing to claw into her face. He imagined he could still see the demoniac eyes of cats, fishbone-teeth bared.

He stood by the south window. He looked out toward the wet yard; the one pane of glass was blurred by streaming water. He didn't look toward the bed and Dossie Bell.

While he anxiously awaited the return of Luster, he had time to think of many things which were closing in on him. He had been at Firbank for ten years. Life had run smoothly and monotonously until the last few months. Dossie Bell's death would change everything.

"I've got to keep ahold of myself. He forced me to come with him and I've got to make the best of it. There's no getting away from him. He must know more than he's letting on. Lord God, what does he want with me? After all my peaceful years, is it going to end like this?"

Brother Lazenby tried to shake off his uneasiness.

If other people would just come over for the sitting-up, things wouldn't be so bad. They would study long and hard before coming to Luster Holder's. And the bad night was a good excuse to stay away.

There were too many tales of what had happened in this section of the hills. These tales went back to the murderous days of John Holder and the Tolby outlaws. Brother Lazenby's every thought of the Nation made him feel smaller and more out of place.

The long grim ride through the woods with the rain beating down, the trees swaying, the lightning crashing had revealed the emotionless character of Luster. Through all the sweeping storm Luster had sat slumped over like a sack of corn, utterly unmoved by the earth's upheaval. He might have been asleep, for all the preacher knew. It just seemed as if he were among something he was used to, that he himself was a part of the storm; or the controller of the storm, he sitting calm and natural, as if sort of bored with the noise of it. He might have been by himself, so far as Brother Lazenby was concerned. He paid no further attention to the minister after they left the schoolhouse.

It was then that Brother Lazenby saw his mistake. There was no use in attempting to escape. Luster would trail him down. He, too, would be found in a ditch with his throat cut.

He shuddered. His sickness was the same which comes to one who longs to be back where everything is familiar.

"I must keep ahold of myself. He mustn't see I'm not myself. I must carry things out like a preacher's supposed to. Maybe he don't know. Maybe he's got his mind set to other things."

Dossie Bell was certainly a pretty woman. Brother Lazenby had known her for several years. He had heard that she came from a distant county. She had been disowned by her people. Old Henley Humphries had befriended her. He had sent her to Auntie Gates' cabin on Cleeburn Creek, where the negro woman took care of her. Sometime later she had gone to live with Luster Holder. Remembrance of these things was vague with the minister. At Firbank he didn't know what to believe. So much was said. What she had told him gave him reason to believe she had been wronged. And he had wronged her with vicious words.

Sunday after Sunday she had come to sit on a front bench at Sobby and hear him preach. She was interested in his sermons even after she had fallen from grace and been churched. The other Nazarenes drew off from her. She sat by herself while folks talked bad things against her scarlet life.

Her name was a blot on the church record, so the member's decided. Brother Lazenby wished to fight for her, to keep her in the fold. He had to think of himself. He couldn't expose his interest in a fallen woman and lose his charge at Sobby.

The day of Dossie Bell's churching was kept as quiet as possible. Only the members knew. Urfie Pearl Buckner was warned not to traipse from house to house with the news. It mustn't reach Luster's ears. Dossie Bell would attend as usual.

On that early spring day all the Nazarenes gathered at Sobby. Brother Lazenby was worried when he saw Henley Humphries and Buck. They had learned despite the caution taken. Henley had come out to defend Dossie Bell. He was a Nazarene but had quit church years before, soon after Brother Lazenby came to Firbank. He had said, "Si, that 'ere Lazenby is a snake in the bosom. He preaches one way and acts another. He may walk the straight and narrow, but hit shore is growed over with brambles and weeds."

Without success Brother Lazenby had tried to reach him. Once Humphries made up his mind about a man there was no changing him. He liked Dossie Bell and meant to see that she was protected. No one, not even the bone-carriers, knew why he took so great an interest in Luster's woman, nor why Buck hung around the cabin with her.

Brother Lazenby recalled that his voice had sounded strangely hollow and foreign as he read the charge. The last words of it lashed him now: "And

we feel that God will never send down His love on
our little flock until Dossie Bell Holder's name is
taken from the book."

She had watched him while he read: her gold-
brown hair in a soft roll at her neck, the overlarge
eyes puzzled, the gentle crescents of her breasts
beneath her white cotton waist. His face had burned
and he was ashamed—ashamed because she trusted
him as her guide, because she would have expected
him to defend her.

Old Humphries' denunciation of the Nazarenes
was like a curse: the old man in baggy overalls, his
needley eyes in a purplish face, the shaking gray
beard. His final fire-words, "Let him which is without no sin cast the first stone at this here helpless little woman!" had left the church-house bleakly quiet.

The vote was taken and she was churched.

He had let them go on with it to save himself.
From that minute he had thought of her in regret.
He had gone to her cabin on the pretext of saving
her for the Nazarenes. He pled with her to throw
off her sin. She listened patiently but refused. She
continued to attend church regularly as if nothing
had happened.

Now in the presence of her dead body he recalled
his last visit to the cabin. His accusation of her stung
him—the unfairness, the deadliness of it. He didn't
wish to remember her as she had been then. Luster
was too near.

He turned from the window. His tall, besoaked form threw a grotesque shadow on the wall. He walked to the bed. The hazy yellowness of the lamp fell on Dossie Bell's upturned face. It left half of it in shadow, as she lay with her neck twisted to one side.

A longing came over him. This woman's being gone left an empty place in his life. He had known she was back in the hills alive. Now she would be in the Sobby graveyard like the others.

He stood for some time looking down at her.

The kitchen door creaked. Luster scolded the dogs.

Back at the south window Brother Lazenby waited.

7

HELLO! HELLO! HELLO!" The voice came out from the blackberry lane, out beyond the sedge-grass on the road banks. Someone was hello-ing the house. Brother Lazenby waited by the window. The harsh voice from the dark broke in upon him like a sudden gunshot. He little knew what next to expect here in Luster's cabin. Already he felt he was being held prisoner alone with Luster and death and tor-turous hours.

Barefooted, Luster stumped to the runway. His feet scraped the floor dryly.

"Who's there?" he bellowed out through the wet black.

"Hit's Squar Kiler, Luster."

"Come in, Square."

Squire Kiler's heavy rubber boots plumped down the dog-run. In the room where Dossie Bell lay, he stopped, leaned his twelve-gauge shotgun against the brick fireplace, threw his wide-brimmed hat into a corner and sat down in the rocking-chair by the north window, stretching out his glistening boots.

The Squire was a big man and gray. His chin whiskers were gray and beaded with water. His eyes were gray and bloodshot. He seemed not to be bothered at all by his dripping yellow corduroy coat and pants. If the walk to Luster's had tired him, he showed no signs of it. He was picking his teeth with a goose-quill stopping by the minute to blow pieces of food hither and yon.

"Miss Sudie tole me you was here, preacher," he said, as if the conversation had been in progress for hours. "I was huntin' you. Of co'se you've heerd what Buck Humphries done to my gal, Birdie. I'll be a-needin' you. I already got the gun and the license. I could marry them, but I 'low I'll be wanted along as a reel witness. Luke he cain't hep me hunt because he's gunnin' fer that 'ere damb sorry Bode Holley. Bode he stole a kaig of Luke's licker and tole some damb lies about a graveyard clean-up. 'y God , them Holleys hain't never brung no ketches in thar backs cleanin' off graves. I don't see why the glorious hell folks want to clean off graves fer noway. I 'low they look better with weeds and grass on them. Luke says he's gonna blow the top offen Bode's head soon as he sees him. Bode Holley sho wouldn't look much bad in a red box with no top on his head. Hit hain't no sight fer sore eyes noway. But that there hain't got nothin' to do with findin' Buck Humphries."

Brother Lazenby put his hands behind his back. With the presence of someone else he drew himself together. "Squire Kiler may be hard," he thought, "but it's a relief to have him here with his loud talk. Anything to break in on Luster Holder. He's chilled the marrow in my bones."

"I have heard, Brother Kiler," he said cautiously. "It is regrettable."

The Squire blew a piece of food toward the face of the clock. "That's one thing certain and two things sho, the son of a bitch has got to marry her. Cain't no young bastard knock-up no daughter of mine and not do right by her."

Nervously Brother Lazenby picked at his coat lapels. But he thought fast, speaking with forced determination. "Yes, he has transgressed God's way. He has sinned against his fellow-man."

"The triflin' peckerwood. His ole man and him's bin makin' threats. The big dog barks and then the little dog barks. Someone was a-sayin' he'd takened out for Kintucky. But I says they hain't never no Humphries'll ever go far. When they gits hungry, they comes back home. I figger he's hid out right down in the river-bottom."

Luster stood by the mantel, his resolute eyes lowered to the Squire. His big hands swung down at his

sides. His body look fagged out, but the unchange-
able quality of his eyes betrayed no fatigue.

The Squire was thinking: "I wish to Christ
Luster'ud set down. But he's got to hear all about
Buck Humphries. He wouldn't give a damb otherwise. Dossie Bell she was crazy as the devil over
Buck, and I guess Luster takened to him right smart-
ly. Goddanged if you kin tell whether Doss is dead
or not by looking at Luster. He allus puts me in the
mind of a dog on a chain, one of them 'ere dogs which
never growls, barks or wags hits tail but is right ready
to pounce at yore throat."

Delicately Brother Lazenby rubbed his hands
together. He cleared his throat. "Buck Humphries
must be punished, Brother Kiler. He must be brought
before the church and let God's children pass judgment upon him. No man can ruin what God has
given and expect to reach the Joy which passeth
all understanding." (Thinking through the fog of
his words: "Why should I be troubled by this news
when I'm already so upset? How can I further betray
Dossie Bell?")

Squire Kiler stood, put on his hat, and picked
up his gun. He was obviously bored. "That fool
preacher'll talk the rest of the night. Hain't nothin'
he likes no better'n hearin' his own voice. He orght
to practice lettin' his tongue rest so his brain'd act."

"Come on, preacher," he rumbled. "Talk's talk.
But gittin' Buck Humphries is another thing. What

you 'low and what is, sho don't bed-up together. I'm tard havin' that gal round the house."

"I'm glad to see you standing by your daughter, Brother Kiler. Blood is thicker than water."

" 'y God, molasses is thicker than water too. Come on!"

Lazenby was glad of the chance to leave the cabin. He wished he were heading out for home and rest. He had no desire to be associated with the Iron Squire. But if he could get away from Luster, it would give him an opportunity to escape from the Squire. He couldn't search for Buck.

He started through the door first.

Someone was climbing the steps.

"It's me," from a small high voice.

Brother Lazenby smiled. He turned to the Squire, who towered behind him. Luster hadn't moved from his place at the mantel, standing as if bolted there.

"It's the wife coming over for the setting-up," he said. He turned back and held out a hand to Sudie. "Come on in, Sudie, I'm glad you've come to help Brother Holder in this awful trouble. It's such a night as tests men's faith." Why had she come way out here? It was no place for a woman, let alone one like Sudie. The presence of Sudie sent his mind back to Dossie Bell. Again he was nauseated.

"How'd you get here?" he asked, coughing.

Sudie smiled. "I see Mr. Holder found you, Winnie. I called Mr. Runnels and he gladly brought me over in his buggy. He went on to see his sick daughter, Emmer Lou, 'cross the river. The road is sure long and rough out here. I never drove over such hills in all my born days. We had to drive in at two places to get out of the worst part of the rain."

Luster stooped over to pull on his shoes.

Sudie threw off the wet black-plush wrap which she had bought in Memphis eight years back. She threw it so the trademark of the Memphis store could be easily seen and read.

"I tried to get here earlier, Mr. Holder," she said as she straightened her dark hair-club with slim graceful fingers. She was taller than Luster remembered her. He'd been seeing so blearily while at her home. Her wide-open yellow-green eyes had a hungry look, as if they lived in longing for something which never quite crossed their vision. The warm, clinging quality of her lips belied the ever-hovering hauntingness of these eyes.

"I tried to get here sooner, Mr. Holder," she said again, seating herself and crossing her black-stockinged ankles. She never looked at anyone while she talked.

Impatiently Squire Kiler waited, his gun tilted against the floor. "We're glad yo're here, Miss Sudie. Me'n the preacher we got to go look fer that scoundrel Buck Humphries." The grayness of the old man was contagious.

Sudie raised her eyes to the Squire, sympathetically.

"I've heard, Square Kiler. I just do know into my time! What's our country comin' to? I do hope you'll find him." She lowered her narrow face into her upstretched hands.

Brother Lazenby cleared his throat, coughed. "He must be punished," he said wearily. "He must be made to face God and confess his guilt."

"Come on, preacher," growled the Squire. "I 'low God'll never see him agin wonst I git my trigger finger workin'." He pushed the minister through the doorway. "He's sho gonna be married fore another sun rises."

Luster listened with passive interest. He didn't say anything as they prepared to leave.

The Squire looked back. "Miss Sudie tole me about Dossie Bell, Luster." For the first time Squire Kiler seemed cognizant of the dead hill-woman. He walked to the bed and looked at her, then at Luster. "Hit's hell, hain't it?" Thar'll be some more folks over 'long t'wards mornin'. Millie, my woman, she'll be a-comin' to hep lay her out. I don't know whur I'll git back 'fore the buryin' or not. I figger so. You'll hafta plant her in a hurry, Luster, wonst the sun comes up. Corpses spile right off these hot times."

They were gone in the darkness.

8

S QUIRE KILER LED the way. Dimly, Brother Lazenby could make out the bulk of his form, moving solidly forward through the night. The Squire took the lane road toward old man Henley Humphries'. "I 'low we better start at taw," he had told the minister.

Brother Lazenby was strong against this, but let himself be led on. He couldn't refuse to go. He didn't want to be out with the profane old Squire. Stories of Kiler came to him: how he had horsewhipped a schoolteacher for keeping Birdie after school when he needed her to pick peas; how he had got drunk on the streets of Melburg, defying the officers to take him to jail. He had stood swaying on Main street shouting, "Hold th' deal!"

"You're goin' to jail," the sheriff told him.

" 'y God, I balk," the Squire said with no hidden meaning. And he did. The sheriff and his deputies had edged away from him. They knew he carried a 32-20 S & W under his belt, that he could fight that a mad bull. It was no mystery how he held his place in the county court. People were afraid to get out and work against him.

The minister remembered how the Squire had treated poor old Aunt Bertha Coonce. She'd owed him for a cord of heater-wood. She died without paying for it, and he levied on the tombstone which the church had bought for her. He had taken it and sold it for the debt.

Squire Kiler had once refused to gather at the church with others and pray for rain during the Great Drought. He had said, " 'y God, you cain't turn Ole Billy's head wonst he gits hit set. [Old Billy was his nickname for God.] He'll start wettin' on us soon and we'll think the bottom's fell outen the durn sky."

The minister hated to be associated with this type of man, but he was glad to be away from Luster Holder. He had no interest in the search for Buck. He must feign an interest because of his church and community. A preacher must always be interested in the things in which his congregation expect him to be interested. This was his life.

Then came back the thought of Luster Holder and Dossie Bell: how they had lived without the marriage vows. Her death had washed everything else clear of his mind. What remained was vague and uncontrollable. He never worried at Sudie's being back there alone with Luster, for when he thought of the cabin, his whole mind became involved with the pretty hill-woman now stilled by death. All previous thoughts of her plagued him.

Rain continued to fall steadily. The air smelled of soaked earth and vegetation.

Old man Henley Humphries was hard to wake. Brother Lazenby reckoned the dead would have finally waked what with the way Squire Kiler banged his gun-butt against the wall and bellowed, "Hello, Henley!" A match grated on an inner wall. Bare feet sounded. Old Humphries appeared in the dog-run, his shadow distorted back of the smoking lamp which he held above his head, extended.

He was enfeebled with his seventy-odd years, his tobacco-stained beard foaming out halfway down his sunken chest. His long fleece-lined drawers stuck tightly to crooked withering legs. He carried a double-barreled shotgun.

"Who's thar?" he asked angrily. "Who's wantin' me at this here hellacious time of night?" White phlegm was mushed in the corners of his squinted eyes.

"Hit's Squar Kiler and Preacher Lazenby. You know what I'm wantin', you damb ole coon!"

Humphries gestured unsteadily with his lamp, sloshing the oil into a beading foam.

"Heber Kiler, either you git yore carkiss offen my land, or I'll blow yore guts all over Neeley County.

My boy he hain't guilty of doin' up yore loose-flingin' slut of a gal. Every who says hit's a goddanged liar. I knowed she'd break a leg the way she's bin ruttin' roun. Buck he hain't nowhur's about here nohow."

Brother Lazenby didn't know what to do in the presence of the raging old man. He stood in abject fear. More than ever he regretted having come with the Squire. He should say something to tide over a bad situation. Humphries had no use for him. He must say something natural. His words sounded pinched and awkward. He was talking all wrong.

"Brother Humphries, we want to do right," he mumbled. "Your boy Buck has done a bad thing. We must make him see his sin and repent."

"Shet up, you yaller-blooded Bibler. Hain't nobody axin you to stick yore feathertopped head in this here."

"Yeh, shut up, preacher," the Squire said shortly. "Quit standin' thar waggin' yore tail like a dog in a meathouse. I'll tend to this here old moth-ate hoss. Ole man," he addressed Humphries, "put up yore far-arms or I'll be puttin' them whar they belongs." He stepped toward Humphries. "Whar's that bastard son of yo'rn at?"

Humphries set the lamp on the floor, tottering. Drops of water spit and crackled against the hot chimney. He raised the shotgun to his shoulder. It wobbled in his infirm grasp.

"Git on!" he yelled hoarsely. "Git on!"

Squire Kiler lunged forward quickly for a man of his size. In a decisive, sweeping movement he struck the gun-barrel upward. The gun exploded, kicking the age-bent man back halfway through the open run. The shots sprinkled high into the cedars before the cabin. A screech-owl fluttered away with an alarmed shriek. Large white drops of water sprayed from the limbs, falling like lead against the hard-packed ground.

The Squire shook Humphries fiercely. He knocked the old fellow flat, and, cursing loudly, left the cabin. He walked down the lane-road, his ears shut to the hysterical cries behind him.

Brother Lazenby had stood as if glued to the ground. His ears sang from the explosion. Only when he saw Kiler leaving did he turn and hurry after him. He knew he had been near death. This was only the beginning. He was frightened but not too much to know he must leave the Squire to his searching and return home.

They stopped at the creek bridge.

Brother Lazenby wished to say something which would gain his escape from the Iron Squire. He was weakened now and feared his words would fail to carry weight. As he looked at Kiler's tall figure, he felt like a little boy once more facing his father. Kiler, utterly imperturbable, treated the Humphries encounter as if he thought it a nightly happening.

"I can't go on, Brother Kiler," the minister said huskily, bleakly. "I'm a peace-loving man. I don't want any more of this trouble. I must return to Brother Holder's cabin. They need me there to help out with Dossie Bell. Sudie needs me. You better continue without me."

Brother Lazenby could imagine the unchanged quality of the Squire's face, that he could see every line of it in the motley dark.

"Le's git on, preacher," he said obdurately, ignoring the plea. "I'm gonna find Buck and thar's goin' to be a weddin' 'fore daybreak. I hain't wantin' you along to do no fightin'. I'll take keer of that end of hit. Co'se a Squar kin marry folks, but I'll be needed as a main witness. If he refuses, thar'll be two buryin's up to Sobby tomorrow stid of one."

Meekly the preacher followed the tall Squire. They climbed and descended the hills, at times feeling their way to keep from running headlong into swinging tangles of muscadine or wildgrape vines. Squire Kiler held his gun in front of him. Brother Lazenby wouldn't touch the trees because of poison-ivy. Even the wind off poison-ivy broke him out badly. When he was a small boy, his mother had taught him a little verse for safety:

> *Leaflets five, live and thrive;*
> *Leaflets three, quickly flee.*
> *Berries red, have no dread;*
> *Berries white, a poisonous sight.*

This was after he had chewed a twig and caught poison-ivy in the mouth. She had cured him with gunpowder and sweetmilk.

A new worry confronted him. Squire Kiler was cutting out of the hills and heading toward the Forked Deer river-bottom. Brother Lazenby thought of the soft oozy grayish-blue bottom clay, the green slimy sloughs; and most of all of the cottonmouth moccasins with their metallic gray, coffin-shaped heads. Cold sweat popped out on his face. Luster Holder was known to walk barefooted all over the low country. He waded the sloughs. He grabbled for fish in the old river-bed, running his hands up under hollow logs. No man could be human and do these things. But some men were born for the woods. They never thought of the dangers. Squire Kiler plowed on through the bushes and seemed to enjoy himself.

After a two-hour walk they emerged from the hills and entered the blackness of the bottom country. Cypress rose darkly in their wake. Brother Lazenby walked more slowly to keep from falling over cypress knees. The wet smell of thick vegetation filled the nostrils. The air was damper, cooler. The rain was a fine drizzle now.

Squire Kiler led on, beating his way through cane-thickets with his gun. Occasionally he stopped to light his pipe, listening. Brother Lazenby could smell the strong homegrown tobacco. There was something strengthening in it even if it did dry his throat and make him cough hackingly. The aroma suggested shelter. He half wished he smoked. He had heard tobacco kept mosquitoes away. With the lessening of rain, numberless mosquitoes whined and whirled around his ears. His face was burning and swelling from their bites.

As a boy he had smoked cornsilk, coffee and grapevine. He liked the soft curlywhite leaves of rabbit-tobacco—life-everlasting. His father had called smoking a sin and whipped him hard with a wagon whip. The grapevine had made his tongue sore. Once at college he had smoked Cubebs for catarrh. It was all right to smoke if you were doing yourself good.

In the canebrakes water ran over the preacher's low-cut shoes. His feet slipped back and forth. He was wringing-wet to his waist. Squire Kiler's rubber boots protected him. He didn't seem to mind the rain. He plunged on and on as if he didn't know anyone was with him.

"That ole fool's afeered," Kiler thought between draws. "He hain't nothin' but a woman. He orght to wear dresses and ruffled drawers. I wonder what a nice woman like Sudie ever tied up to him for. I wouldn't a-brought him draggin' along but he kin marry them right short off when I find the bastard and git him back to my house."

Big gray owls vaulted from limb to limb above their heads. A wildcat screamed-out across the river. Chilled and fatigued, the minister thought of turning and working back toward the hills. He didn't know the way. He couldn't afford to get lost in this slush-country at night. He thought of sitting down to wait for day. He didn't care to be alone.

The swamps, gathering black and glistening, made him feel a creeping loneliness, an unnaturalness, like when he'd seen old man Cobey Barker's body drawn up out of a cistern, wet and corpse-green.

They slushed through backwater and neared the river. On the banks of the Forked Deer they found an old cypress log and sat down.

"We'll build a little far here and dry up," said the Squire. "I 'low we'll haft to wait'll hit lights up 'fore we kin go any further. You sorter look petered, preacher."

From his place on the log Brother Lazenby watched the Squire pull dead branches off a water-oak to build a fire. He was very much relieved to be settled after the grueling walk. The spot was far from desirable, but anything was better than onward plunging through unknown sloughs. He made no move to help Kiler. He was too tired and sore. The walk from Luster's cabin was the hardest work he ever remembered doing. It was as if all the hard labor he was to do on earth had been reserved for one night, the worst possible night.

Squire Kiler soon had a blaze started. He sat down and dried his hands. He took a pint of whis-ky from his coat pocket and drank two-thirds of it. He handed the remainder to the preacher. Brother Lazenby refused the bottle, pushing it from him with unsteady hands. He shook his head. "I need it," he was thinking. "I need a drink of spirits if I ever did on earth, but I can't break over. And I can't lower myself by drinking with this man. I must uphold myself without the aid of it."

He said wearily, "I never touch the poison stuff, Brother Kiler. It makes brutes of men. It cankers the soul. It tears the tissues of the body and burns them up like kindling-wood. You must quit before it's too late."

Squire Kiler grunted. "Hit burns the guts and lets the soul take keer of hitself. But I hain't beggin' nobody to drink none of my licker. I kin allus find room for more."

Against his will, Brother Lazenby went on in subdued tones, not very much interested while his thoughts were on other prodding things. In his insecurity he wished to make conversation, with the forlorn hope that in the sound of a human voice he would forget his dread surroundings. He knew his words were lost on the Squire.

"Yes, but, Brother Kiler, the Great Creator has said in Corinthians 6:10 that a drunkard shall not inherit the Kingdom of God."

The Squire grunted. "I hain't wantin' to inherit no kingdom of God. I got enough to do here on earth lookin' after my bottom farm."

He drained the bottle and tossed it into the river.

Brother Lazenby studied him for a long time in awe, seeming unable to say anything more. The bright light from the fire and the pleasant warmth strengthened him momentarily. At last he asked, "Brother Kiler, do you believe a woman who sins with a man like Dossie Bell Holder did will ever get to Heaven?"

With a thumb Squire Kiler worked fresh tobacco into his pipe.

"I says a woman which hain't did like Dossie Bell Holder done sho-God has missed-out on her livin'."

"Yes, but Brother Kiler, it's the law of God and man which she has broken," he said, disheartened, futile.

"I hain't got not time for no law. I says if a man does what he figgers is right, hit's right. Hit's right for him and wy should he be worryin' whether hit's right for anybody else. You sho-God let little things plague you, preacher."

Brother Lazenby sat quietly, resignedly, shaking his head.

"You see, preacher," the Squire said, chuckling, as if he were explaining to a little child, "a woman was made to do what us men says do. If we says, 'Frog!' she's supposed to jump right short off. A woman's gonna do wrong whether hit's with her body or not. If hit ain't her body, hit'll be her mind. Her tongue'll be loose at both ends and flappin' in the middle. She'll do her dirt with hit."

Brother Lazenby said nothing else. He reasoned laboriously: "The Squire sits here talking one way while he's acting another. He cares nothing for Birdie. He loves trouble. He never is better satisfied than

when mixed up in trouble. He's had more lawsuits
than anybody else in Neeley County. He just wants
to get Birdie off his hands. If he wasn't out after Buck,
he'd be out after somebody else."

Squire Heber Kiler was made of iron. The
tough-fibered old man betrayed no signs of fatigue.
The preacher didn't want to find Buck Humphries.
Thoughts of his own life at seventeen made him
ashamed he was helping track down a mere boy. He
couldn't do anything further against Dossie Bell.

He feared for Buck and wished strongly for him
to elude this torment of a man who stalked him so
relentlessly. Out here in this black country it was
impossible to hitch blame on the boy. He only held
against Buck that he never attended church. He had
talked to Buck without success. Buck listened attentively, saying little, and then did just exactly as he
had always done.

He had never heard of Buck's doing any other
wrong than to not attend church. Buck was quiet and
moody. He acted old for his age. Didn't anybody like
him or his old pappy. Some said he was crazy; that his
life was built out of evil. People said this of anyone
they couldn't understand. Buck was not a Christian,
but he never had disturbed the preacher's meetings.
He had never slipped up, drunk, and thrown rocks
on the church roof to drown out the minster's voice.
He had never ridden by with a bunch of louts, whoop-
ing and firing pistols into the air.

Birdie Kiler attended church regularly. Brother Lazenby had never talked with her. He had heard tales which he partly believed. It was in her favor that she came to hear him preach.

All of it was puzzling to the minister.

Squire Kiler was dozing, his head leaned forward in his hands. Brother Lazenby's thoughts returned him to Luther's cabin. Sudie was there for the sitting-up, alone with Luster unless others had braved the night. He saw Dossie Bell again as she sat through her churching, never raising a word in her defense.

He saw her in the cabin as he had pled with her.

With Luster Holder she had removed herself from the minster's world. And he had endeavored to break into her life, to change it against her will. For her he was willing to jeopardize his own standing, to drive himself to desperate things.

Luster wasn't his kind. He took no part in the troubles of the church and settlement. He had kept Dossie Bell from it. He led a hard, dangerous, god-forsaken life of his own. But why had he let her be churched? Would he remember her hurt and seek revenge on those who had wronged her?

Dossie Bell's death, the draggling night and the ruthless Squire had changed the minister. Had he failed as a child of the Lord? His own father had told him he was cut out to carry God's word to even the least of them. His whole life had been shaped for the work. How could he give it up? In church he was on his own ground and respected.

Tonight he was assailed by doubt, doubt of his own faithfulness in view of what had happened.

He forgot the wet night, the Squire. He gazed steadily at the glowing coals. Because he had reached an ending after his long tedious years at Firbank, he sought to pause and look back on all which had gone before. His past descended upon him as if spun out of the isolating darkness of the swamps. He reviewed it, projecting himself into it painfully; recalling its drabness; thinking in self-pity of the brutality of his father.

His whole life seemed like nothing that had ever actually happened, like a story he might have read.

There was Conway Lazenby, his stern father, an Arkansas farmer who distrusted his fellowman and loved God. Brother Lazenby lived to be guided by his father's will. He remembered the hot drives with his parents to arbor meetings in the squeaky buggy, dust rising in a thin gritty cloud to whiten their clothes and settle over adjacent corn and cotton fields.

From the beginning he had been told that he was born to preach. His father had at one time in his life received the call from God. A constant struggle with the soil had kept him from becoming a minister. God had given him a son who would fulfill the call. Old Conway's words returned to Brother Lazenby now, "The mantle I was to of wore falls on you, Winnie." They had knelt around the kitchen table and prayed the call into him: Brother Klabert, the Nazarene revivalist; his father, and Clinthea, his ever-remembered-as-silent mother. After hours he was named as one of God's voices. He had begun reading and memorizing Scripture. His father helped him, praying over him threateningly if he failed. Although he was afraid of being a minister, he never rebelled after he knew his career was cut out for him. Only once he had told his father, "I'm afraid, Pappy."

"Afeered of what?" the old man demanded.

"I'm afraid of God." God had been pictured to him as a harsh man, not unlike Conway Lazenby, who watched his every move and read his every thought before it was formed.

"You'll preach God, Winnie," the old fellow said hotly. "I'll conquer you or kill you. You was made to preach. Me and yore ma has tried to do right by you. We don't think you'll betray yore trust. I'd rather see you stretched out in yore coffin than to think you'd ever do it."

This decided him. He never again rebelled.

He had looked upon his father as a stanch Christian, a strong Bible-man of the Old-Time-Religion school. Conway was a power on whom to lean. Later in life he learned things of the old man which he never believed: that he had stuffed ballot-boxes in county elections; he had drowned a negro by throwing him into the Cache River with an anvil tied to his feet; from his own gin he had sold cotton which had large stones in the center of the bales.

He recalled his three months at Junior College. He hadn't liked the atmosphere of college. Schooling kept his ideas scattered and away from the Book. Preaching was only to be learned through preaching. He returned home and took up his duties at various Nazarene churches. He became known as the Boy Wonder Preacher of Eastern Arkansas. Over an oil-lamp, late at night, his father wrote his sermons. Winnie memorized them while one or the other of his parents held the paper to prompt him. One Sunday he would preach before an arbor crowd in some little back-in-the-swamps community; the next at a river gathering for all-day services where he delivered a sermon both morning and afternoon. He liked to give these sermons. He despised preparing and memorizing them.

His reputation as a soul-saver spread. And one summer he was called to hold a revival meeting at the Sobby church in West Tennessee. He crossed the river to stay a month, and ten years had passed. During the Sobby meeting he met Sudie Steel, also from Arkansas, who was teaching school at Firbank. They met at Urfie Pearl Buckner's chicken barbecue. Like himself, Sudie was a great worker in the church. She was drawn-in and shy. Once together they seemed to see that their lives ran in the same course. He saw her as a useful helper in his work. She could take the place of his father and mother.

He never loved her. He had never loved anyone, so it didn't matter. Before the meeting was over he had asked her to be his wife.

The Sobby Nazarenes liked Winnie Lazenby. He became their regular pastor and settled with his wife near the church-house.

He could never understand Sudie nor had he cared to. She was not like what he thought a wife would be. Her interest was in the church rather than the home. They lived like strangers although she was kind and considerate of him in many ways. They attended church together and worked as one for the Nazarene cause. But at home they were distant and seldom talked except when others were present. She was more like a sister who cared for and watched after him. She admired him as a man of God.

Only his sermons brought them together. She wrote his weekly sermon and helped him memorize it. She sat on the front bench at Sobby and prompted him when he forgot.

Ten dragging years had passed; ten years of isolation among the Tennessee hillmen from Seven Ridges to the Big Survey. He was tired long before Dossie Bell came to Firbank and joined the church. When he first saw her, he began to realize the monotony of his life. The little woman sent his thoughts to roving. She put new power into the way he delivered his sermons. He looked forward to each Sabbath day.

Then the congregation learned of Dossie Bell's life with Luster Holder. Against his will Brother Lazenby had led them in turning her from the church. She had continued to attend, but he was not himself when he faced her.

He had sent women of the church to beg her to give up her sinful ways so that she might be reinstated. They had failed. He began his own secret missions to her cabin. He called it duty to the church, to God, to save her before it was too late. In his heart he knew differently. Only one thing would cause him to slip through the woods to the hill cabin when he knew Luster was far away. For the first time in his life he desired a woman. In his passion for her he forgot his fear of God's wrath, his father's warning, Sudie, and danger. If he had betrayed his trust, he didn't care.

His early training had come to nothing. Tomorrow he would stand before the hill-folks and say words over her cold body. What, he had no idea. And that big brown man would be there to hear.

Very much dejected, in the bleakness of the bottom night, Brother Lazenby sat on the riverbank and forgot the time, the place, the Squire, in the bitter thoughts of a spent life.

Squire Kiler's words fell upon him, harshly breaking into his living past. Heber Kiler had stretched to his feet and picked up his gun.

"Come on, preacher. Hit's nigh day. We got to find a trail."

A first faint silver strip nestled along the horizon to announce the closing of the night. A steel-gray sky began to show through the sheen of fine rain. Dripping trees were wet-green, their trunks black, shining, steaming, scarcely taking form through the foglike drizzle. Water dripped from soggy limbs and click-clicked into thick matty grass beneath them. Out over the river a white blanket was spreading like wood-smoke until it melted away into the dank grayness toward Melburg. The river was rising, its water in brown, trash-flecked whorls.

Brother Lazenby's clothes touched his cold limbs unpleasantly. Mist gathered in tiny balls on the ends of his eyelashes. He smeared it off with the edge of his sleeve. He was stiff and sore.

He followed the Squire, who was fast breaking his way through a clump of blackberry bushes.

9

L USTER SAT DOWN in the rocking-chair opposite Sudie Lazenby and took off his shoes. He
rubbed his cramped feet. He yawned, although he
was not sleepy now: sleep had left him somewhere
back in the rainy night. It was past midnight, the latest he remembered sitting up in years. He had stayed
at his still, but slept off and on, a jug of white whisky at his elbow; just keeping wide enough awake to
regulate the fire.

He raised his emotionless gray eyes to the woman
who sat opposite him, like he might be looking at
the clock, the dark marble-topped bureau, or Dossie
Bell, cold on the bed. She was watching him, damp-
ening her lips with the tip of her tongue. When he
caught her eyes, she lowered them to the ends of her
patent-leather pumps.

"Hit's right nice of you to come, Miss Lazenby," he said dryly, as if it were an accident he had spoken at all; his words tuned so they might cause her to go off somewhere and leave him to himself.

She was reminded of her presence far out in the Nation's hills.

"Ain't it awful, Mr. Holder?" she faltered. "Dossie Bell was such a purty woman. It puts me all back in the mind of another day and time." The vacantness of her voice startled her as it broke through the feebly lighted room. She added absently, "We'll lay her out so soon as the others get here. The night's been so bad and all."

Luster made no comment. He continued to stare wearily at her, his face wooden. Her warm-looking lips were drawn in tightly against her teeth. He could see the glint of gold on one tooth.

Silence bore in on them. Late night dulled the lamp's beams to sickly green. The lamp was like time suspended: the oil, low in the big bowl, seemed never to go any lower, its wick drinking no longer. It held back the lives of the two who sat before it and made them seem as dead as she who lay in the corner.

Luster watched her while appearing to have no thought of her presence, his stare contagiously cold, impersonal. His bare feet pressed soundly against the floorboards. His clothes, still wet, hung in dark wrinkles on his lithe body. Hair fell in a mop near his eyebrows and covered his smooth forehead. Large-knuckled hands lay uselessly in his lap.

She wished strongly to break the flat, endless silence. She thought of her very aloneness here with Luster Holder: this Godless Holder man who never had been saved. "If I had only known how it would be. I'm uneasy, but I don't want to leave. Others will surely come over. I wanted to come after I saw him tonight. I don't know what urged me on. I had to see him.

"He's so quiet, but there's something like fire under it. He's like a part of everything out here. No wonder people fear him. Winnie should be back soon, though there's no telling when they'll find Buck Humphries.

"I can't sit here this way all night. I've got to say something to him. I never felt so jerky and queer in all my life. I'll scream if he don't move. I never saw anyone like him. I can't keep my eyes from his. Some hidden power in them is drawing me and putting a spell over me. I must say something."

She thought painfully, proving her mind for a subject.

When she spoke, the words came from an almost motionless mouth, pushed from back in her throat in broken waves.

"I'd say you better change your wet clothes, Mr. Holder. You'll catch your death of cold." She stopped short, awed by the tonelessness, the haunting hollowness of her voice. "It don't sound like me talking," she thought, aware of a sudden dizziness. "Am I changing into somebody else? Is this whole queer experience to break me from what I've been?" She bit her lips, alarmed by a rising idea, and idea which increased in strength at each recurrence.

He continued to look at her with monotonous indifference.

"I figger I better had," he drawled carelessly, impassively. Without taking his eyes from her he backed into the kitchen adjoining and closed the door.

In the moist dark he stood for minutes near the dining-table. The smell of spoiled food rose to his nostrils. Leisurely he pulled the soggy jumper from his arms and threw it into a corner. His blue shirt ripped as he slipped it from his shoulders. His overalls fell to the floor and he stepped out of them, on them, leaving them crumpled at his feet. He took a short sack towel from a wall nail and dried his wet limbs. He filled his lungs with stifling air, expelling it by sinking them fast.

He pushed open the outside door. It was drizzling again, although the moon shone intermittently. Mist spit against his face. He hunted over the room and found a clean pair of overalls. He pulled them on without a shirt.

At the door to the big-room he paused. He seemed just to realize Sudie Lazenby was in there. She was in there with Dossie Bell, the woman her husband had wanted him to bring out of the hills and marry. He had never known Sudie Lazenby. Death had brought her into his life.

"I wasn't needin' no help out there. Dossie Bell she always thought a body'ud hafta have a preacher around to git them into Heaven. I be damn if I kin see why. Her death come on me so quick and I was so tard, I wasn't shore what to do. Miss Lazenby's eyes was queer when she put them on me. She don't look as peaceful-like as when I seen her at her house. Why the hell didn't she stay home like the others done if she's afeered? But she's a right purty woman even if she is skeered. And Dossie Bell she's dead."

He stood close to the big-room door with his hand on the knob. When he opened it, she still sat where he had left her. She glanced up, her face reddening, as if she had been watching the door for his reappearance. Her slim body seemed to melt down into the chair. Her lips moved, but she didn't speak. Her breath came in short gasps. She fiddled her fingers in her lap.

She watched him steadily as he walked toward her. She was unable to turn her head from him. When he stopped by her chair, she rose to face him. His eyes were on her meditatively. She searched them in an amazement akin to fright and seemed to discover something which fascinated her.

His voice was low. "Come out to the kitchen." The words rang in her ears, deafened her. She followed him into the dark room as if powerless to do otherwise.

10

BUCK HUMPHRIES WAITED through the threatful night, his back against a maple sapling. He saw the smoke from the fire across the river. It must be Squire Kiler's fire. He never thought of anyone, let alone Brother Lazenby, being with him.

For two days and nights, seemingly endless, Buck had hidden out beyond the Forked Deer. He had gunned his food, killing rabbits and squirrels, quail and doves. He had tried to sleep on the hard ground. Most of the time he had lain on his back, his head in his coupled hands, watching the shimmering blue of the summer sky. This night he had watched a cold gray void, the chill of the earth creeping into the joints of his frail body. He had waited in continual dread.

His leather boots and corduroy trousers were caked with gray clay, his khaki hunting-coat torn by thorns and matted with green burrs he hadn't troubled to pick off. His face was drawn by the expectancy of something grave to happen. A two-day growth of downy stubble made him feel older than his seventeen years.

Squire Kiler was on his trail and would kill him if he didn't marry Birdie. He had hated to leave home. His father had sent him into the bottom country. He wanted to be near Old Henley, braved by the presence of the aged man. Alone, he had too much time to think of the rugged Squire and to build on a situation which left him weak and puzzled. His greatest fear was of Birdie herself, the thought of having to marry her.

All through the rain-swept night he sat while a yellowish red glare rose from Kiler's fire. The Squire's patient waiting was slowly driving him to desperation. Sooner or later he would be found. He didn't have any idea what he'd do then.

He hadn't looked for trouble. He was seldom with people. Most of his time was spent with his pappy. Old Henley was not curious and meddling even if he did frighten the boy with his tales of early lawless days in West Tennessee and the visions which he had seen. The old fellow's stories cause him to forget his great unhappiness: the whispered things he didn't understand, while realizing that a damaging secret hung above him.

Not many Nationites cared for him. The Nazarenes had it in for him because he wouldn't come to the meeting-house. Crowds nauseated him, whether at Sobby or Melburg; they made him feel sneaking and conscious of a shrouding timidity. He couldn't face them as did Luster Holder, a man who was never more alone than when surrounded by men. He couldn't face Luster. There was something of raw power and suggestive savagery about Luster which made Buck wish to crawl into a hole and drag it in after him.

He admired Luster at a distance. He knew of his Cherokee blood. It turned one's mind back to other days—of silent trails, of Chickasaws, Shawnees and Cherokees fighting for possession of the Western District; stalking deer and bear. Luster's grandfather had gone bear hunting with David Crockett up in the Shakes country around Reelfoot Lake. Luster had a knife which once belonged to the Colonel.

Buck liked to think he was a man of the woods, a man who inspired respect. He could never be. Even now he was fleeing from Old Squire Kiler, in constant fear Kiler would find him and drag him back, helpless, to Firbank to marry his daughter. He would be shot down like a dog if he refused. And nothing would ever be done about it.

He tried not to think of death. But he did worry about death and God. He believed in God, but not the God of Brother Lazenby and Sobby. He liked to sit and listen to Old Henley read and explain the scriptures, even if the weird explanations and visions worried him so he lay awake at night. Henley Humphries had built up his own way of approaching God. He stayed away from Sobby and "the mess and noise of the churchers." He believed the parts of the Bible which he thought suitable to his religious needs. With a red crayon he had marked out the passages which he didn't like.

He needed no one to explain. It was no different when he was a boy, and he saw no need of talking over it and mending on it continually. One man's opinion on it was as good as another's; your own was better for you.

He liked the country as it was when he was young. He fought good roads because they brought in trash. During the war he had been against Daylight Saving and refused to tamper with his clock. "What God has started off," he said, "shouldn't orght to be changed. He knowed best. Si, the gov'ment cain't fool me."

He told Buck of how the world was made. It was flat as a flitter and if you walked far enough you reached the jumping-off place. Every night God sent out angels to light the stars. They carried flaming pine-knots and stuck them to coaloil-soaked stars. The sun was a big globe which was lighted up like a lamp. It took a thousand gallons of oil to run it through one day. Over a hundred angels hoisted it on their shoulders and carried it across the heavens. The moon shone out occasionally so that God could see how sinners did at night.

Any unusual question from the boy brought the same answer. "Hit's not fer me to know. That 'ere's one of God Almighty's myst'ries."

His father knew more of explaining the Bible than did Brother Winnie Lazenby. There was something unnatural—brought-on—in the way the minister preached. He talked as if he were a little uncertain of the things he explained. He lacked the power of believing which Buck's pappy had: Old Henley told his off as if it could be no other than true. He had Scripture of his own—chimney-corner Scripture.

Thoughts of Old Henley's God came to Buck strongly now that he was a fugitive from the wrath of the Godless Heber Kiler. Buck had had faith in his pappy's Lord, but would He protect him from the Squire? He, too, read his Bible, a Red Letter Bible given to him by Dossie Bell. He believed in keeping God's word. He cringed to think of how Squire Kiler blasphemed the Holy Ghost. When it rained, the Squire would rush from his house shaking his fist at the sky, shouting, "Rain, damb you, rain!" Buck would have feared a lightning-flash, for lightning was the Fire of God. This explained why a barn or house struck by lightning couldn't be extinguished.

Brother Lazenby had talked to Buck and asked him to come to church. Only in church, he explained, can you hope to reach the Joy which passeth all understanding. The minister cautioned him and told him many stories of the sudden deaths of those who had refused the Nazarene word. The stories weakened

Buck, but his pappy had hooted them away. "That 'ere danged Lazenby," he said, "don't amount to not more than a hiccup in a whirlwind. He'll never git no nigher Heaven than Hell's front gate."

The gossips said Buck was crazy, that there was a secret about his birth. No one knew his mother and talk said Henley Humphries wasn't his father. Urfie Buckner said he was a unbeknownst orphant which Old Henley had taken in. There were strange, unfounded tales about his mother. Henley never mentioned her only to say she was the best woman on God's earth. Buck heard the fantastic tales and they bewildered him. They left their mark of unhappiness on him. He never questioned his father; for, despite the gossip, he accepted Henley as father.

With the Birdie Kiler trouble, the stories were revived. Buck had led her astray. Birdie, on a sudden, became to many of them a pure girl victimized. Whatever they knew to be the truth, Buck Humphries must be put in his place. They talked of forming a party and waiting-on him and his pappy. As this talk grew, Henley sent Buck into hiding.

"Git to the woods, Buck," he ordered. "Si, shoot the first son of a bitch whicht comes atter you. A Humphries hain't axin' fer no mercy and shore hain't givin' none."

"I cain't, Pappy," Buck plead." I'm afeered. I want to be with you."

"They'll find you here, boy. You cain't stay."

"I'm skeered to be off by myself in them woods knowin' he's on my trail."

Old Humphries had grasped him by the arms and shaken him. "You'll git. I hain't gonna have no Humphries a-showin' yaller. Git 'fore I lose my temper."

Buck had left the house, heavy-hearted, trying to keep his pappy from seeing he was about to cry. The last he saw of Humphries he was standing in the cabin runway, his long beard moving up and down as he chewed.

Henley had tried to teach Buck how to fight: cutting, gouging, stamping. "Si, the quickest way of gittin' a feller is best," he explained. "The sooner he's whooped, the better fer him. Si, hit sometimes saves killin's."

Buck didn't like fighting. Once, overcome with anger, he had knifed a Melburg boy for turpentining his dog. The flow of blood had sickened him.

Squire Kiler intended unloading Birdie on him. It must be someone, so he had picked Buck because the Humphries owned land, were pretty well fixed. And Buck would be easy to handle. She would settle down after marriage. He didn't care, just so he was rid of her. Buck knew of the Kilers' negro blood. It was common knowledge in Neeley County. Squire Kiler's grandfather had been a big, blue-glummed, yellow-eyeballed negro, so folks said.

Birdie was her father made over. Buck had heard remarks at the store:

"She's the passionest heifer a-breathin'."

"She's the hottest thing in Neeley or anywhere's else, 'y God. She swinges ever'thing she passes."

Buck hated to hear talk against her. He was sorry for Birdie and thought a lot of her even if her presence did unnerve him. It wasn't right to slander a girl.

Birdie had sent him "sweet hello" one day at school, little Ossa Simms running clear across the schoolyard to whisper it in his ear. He had never given her a thought until then. He considered the dark curly-haired girl much older than himself. She was loud-talking, always laughing out in time of books of passing notes to the boys.

Buck's face had burned when one of her notes came to his desk. It read:

Bucky honey—I'm jus goin to waist waiting for you, sugar pie. We was made for each other. See me soon.
        Birdie xxxxxxxxxx

He dreaded to look at her after this. She was just making fun of him because he was puny. He dodged her on the school grounds and cut through the woods to keep from walking down the road with her.

But by himself in the woods his thoughts would return to her: the swell of her red lips, the dark mystery of her eyes, the grace of her well-turned body as she walked—the ease and poise of a bobcat. The very things which drew him to her, scared him. He dared never be alone with her. Her deep voice was too careless. She seemed ever to be searching for words to cheapen herself.

His date with Birdie was by accident. He was driving home late from Melburg. At the forks of the road near the Refuge schoolhouse he saw a girl leaning against the wagon-wheel on which the mailboxes were nailed. In the light of the full moon he recognized Birdie. She leaned languidly on her elbow, standing hipped.

When he recognized her, he sensed his body tauten, then grow weak. He decided to drive on by. She waved for him to stop.

"Hidy, Birdie," he said unevenly, his heart drumming. He wondered what she could be doing alone and so far from home. She had had a late date and was walking home so her father wouldn't catch up with her, he supposed. Or had she been waiting for him, knowing he must pass Refuge on his return from the county seat?

"Move over, Becky," she said, laughing so her teeth flashed in the moonlight. She climbed into the buggy beside him, her loose dress pulling back under her as she plopped down, revealing legs, milk-white.

The night was oppressively hot for spring. Buck's horse was just lifting his feet, barely dragging the buggy after him. Particles of dust like puffs of silver filled the air. Frequently the horse stopped to eat a sprig of grass in the narrow lane. The lane was cut-out in chalk by the moon. Roadside bushes snapped and scraped against the buggy spokes; low-hanging branches brushed and rubbed the buggy top.

Buck opened no conversation. He didn't know how to talk to her. He had been with girls few times before and never with one like Birdie. He was anxious to get her home. Stories of her filled his mind.

"Yo're a funny feller, Bucky," she said, edging closer. He felt the warmth of her hips through her damp cotton dress.

He didn't say anything. He kept his eyes on the horse's rising and falling rump. He could imagine the oval of her face, a jeering, witch-face.

She reached for his hand and held it against her knee, her heating eyes raised to him. He had to look into their opaqueness, awed, being drowned in them.

"Yo're the foolishest feller I ever seen," she said, a little like she was mad. "You got 'bout as much sense as a last year's bird's nest."

He never moved when she called "Whoa!" to the horse. Something held him rigid, still bewitched. The horse paused and ate leaves from a low limb. Birdie put her arms around Buck's neck and pulled his head down. She sank her lips into his, drawing into them, her breath moist and hot. He pulled her close, held between his fulling passion and a dread chill which racked him.

"Well, do something, fool," she panted. "Yo're green as gourd guts!"

She begged him to come see her. He never did. He tried to keep her from his mind, to forget all which had happened, fighting to lose the image of her body in the moonlight. He couldn't face her.

When she found herself with child, she was quick to say it was his.

It might be. Buck didn't know. There were others to whom it could belong. Birdie may have loved him. He doubted she was the type to love anyone for long. He fought off a certain love for her which had grown out of the memory of the night.

He longed to see Dossie Bell again. He loved the pretty hill-woman. Since he was a little boy he had stayed with her as much as possible. He had gone to her with his troubles, when his heart was sick with the ugly stories of the community; when he was the victim of the bonecarriers—the gossips. She caused him to ignore the Firbank gabblers. She tried to keep him from being shy of Luster Holder. The big hill-man never said a word to him. And this silence was worse than harsh words. The cold eyes seemed to stare out in resentment against Buck's visits. Buck tried to pick the days when Luster was not at home.

He needed her now and couldn't go to her.

The rain-drenched breeze off the river drove night swiftly by Buck's eyes. And always there was more of it, passing endlessly.

"I cain't tell whether I love Birdie," he kept thinking. "I know I cain't never marry her. I'm sorry for anyone who was cut out from the beginning to be

what she is. She couldn't git out of it. Me and her ain't
of a kind. No child from me could be hers. What's
hers is tainted with her. It'll be her over again. It
makes my stomach sick to think how helpless she
is to be anything different. It was decided for her
before she was borned.

"I've dirtied myself. I'm poisoned from her. That
night undid me. What I'd been for years was takened
away. I couldn't mention it to Dossie Bell even if I
seen her. She'd never think the same of me again.
She'd look on me as unclean.

"But I guess she knows it now like ever'body over
the Nation settlement. She's at her cabin thinkin' her
disappointment in me, of how I've drug myself down
to the equal of niggers.

"I cain't go to her."

The rain worried him: its monotonous dripping,
its sogging and melting everything together. He
wished it would break off.

11

THE KILER HOME was in a grove of oaks not far from Goddard's store at Firbank: an old two-story house whose paint had crumbled off and left the weatherboarding brown and dilapidated. Following the night's rain it looked strangely deserted. Ominously dark clouds hung low over its moss-slickened roof. Virginia-creeper grew heavily on one end of the house, climbing from twisting roots underneath the floor. Smoke rose from the covering of leaves, for no chimney was visible. Green-and-gold chinaberry trees were bunched to one side of the narrow porch.

In the yard flower-beds of cannas, sunflowers and prince's-plumes drooped in bright dripping color. Garret and Bruton snuff-bottles surrounded these beds, stuck into the ground, bottoms-up. Millie Kiler was saving a pile of jars at the corner of the house to circle her grave. The Kiler dead had snuff-bottles around their mounds. Also she was saving broken pitchers, broken plates—anything broken and beyond use at the house, like lamp-bowls, shaving-mugs, cups, saucers, percolater tops, Mason-jar tops and lemon-squeezers—to decorate graves. When she was laid to rest under the ragged cedars of the Sobby churchyard, she'd be happy to know her grave was prettied-up like the rest.

Birdie was in the kitchen with her mother. She sat in a cornshuck-bottomed chair by the kitchen stove. In a foreboding silence she watched Millie, who sat by the cook table with a dishpan of whippoorwill peas, her blue-veined hands shelling steadily.

Birdie was thinking of other things. Her eyes were red and puffed. Her olive skin gave an outside darkness to her whole body. Curly hair bushed out over her head, uncombed. Beneath her cotton dress she could feel unborn life. With each feel of it she experienced the threat of ending time. She, kept at home by her father since the Buck Humphries' trouble, imagined disturbing things: the shortness of the pleasure she had known; the suddenness of misery come to hang on forever.

She had been called wild as the winds, one ever on the go. On the go day after day. She had never known anything else. At home she was restless as a dog straining at its leash. And now she was stopped short, folded up here and held by a raging father.

To be cooped up at home was prison to her. She felt if she could be gadding over the hills, she would forget her trouble and again be herself. If she could go to one place and be there forever, she knew life again would be promising.

Her mother didn't talk. She feared Birdie's outbursts. For days she had tried to keep the subject from her mind: to think of living things while death images pursued her. She had never thought of death for herself until now. She was built for work, toil and toil with never the time to stop and think why. Work was her reason for living. She rode with a whip from morning until night. Death was something which came to others, she existing to see them pass away, existing to slave for Heber Kiler.

The snuff-bottles were saved because she knew how pretty they made a grave look. They kept ghosts away from the dead. In their charmed circle one could rest in peace, rest up gloriously until the sounding of the Big Horn. She had given bottles to her friends. In her fifty-five years Millie figured she had dipped-up enough bottles of snuff to circle every grave at Sobby.

She had thought death, but for other people. She was beholden to Heber Kiler. Only when he released her could she think of eternal rest.

Even before she knew Squire Kiler, there had been toil: her sharecropper father had moved from place to place, managing badly. One year he had farmed the poorest of red-clay hills and drought burned up the crops; another year found him on the edge of the bottom and the overflowing river would wash out the cotton and corn. Her grandfather, Old Artie Tolby, had once owned all the Nation lands. Her father had gambled away what little was left. His children had done the work, provided the food which they ate: salty sowbelly, hoecakes and sorghum molasses most of the year around.

Her hard life had never been a memory, never ceased long enough to become a memory. With her father she had known the worst of field work: in spring, following the plow until her hands were calloused, her arches so sore from stepping on clods that she had to put crushed newspaper into her shoes; summer, wet with sweat, pitching hay into high-boarded wagons while sweat bees danced before her burning, aching eyes; fall, cotton in the fields, pick-sack swinging from her shoulders, fingers broken open, blackened, cuticle torn: on her knees picking; winter, with frightfully cold winds scouring up from the river, beating through cracks in the walls, whipping loose the cardboard window coverings.

She had never figured it wasn't a woman's work. She grew into it. And when she married Heber she knew what to expect. Heber had money and owned a lot of timberland. He had sold enough whisky to float half of Neeley County and overflow the other half, so folks said. He still dabbled in it although he was a member of the county court. He let the negroes on his bottom place make it. When a still was found by officers from Melburg—which was seldom—a negro always went along to explain how it got there. Folks over Neeley said the Squire's whisky was good as the best charred stuff in West Tennessee, but high as a cat's back.

She married Heber. He still told around the Firbank store that when he took her off her father's hands, she didn't have anything but what he wanted and a Bible. And the Squire figured the Bible was as useful as a side-saddle for a hog.

It was the working, the drudging for life: life meant it. The escape from the sharecropper years with her father meant their continuation with the Squire.

She expected no pay or thanks for her work, for she had never received either. He raged and found fault with everything. All of this through the years until she came to believe it was right. She cringed from him ever in the expectation of something awful to happen, the not happening of it somehow a disappointment. It was as if she always waited for the worst and was put-out when it didn't appear.

Millie had thought of death for others. This was before the Birdie-Buck trouble, a trouble which had thrown the house from a big hell to a bigger hell—a hell which set her to thinking thoughts suggestive of death; caused her to mutter to herself over and over, "I've shore reached the jumpin'-off place at last."

Death all at once became a near reality. Dark and overshadowing, it hovered above her as she did her daily work. It followed her to bed and stayed so near she couldn't sleep, smothering-spells causing her to beat the air for breath.

Of nights, when she went alone to the barn to milk, she saw topas—the shadows of death—scurrying at her side. Sometimes they were as big as the palm of her hand, and again as large as a calf. She had hooted at the idea when an old negress told her of having a terrapin conjured into her stomach. Now she feared that death in the form of a topa had been conjured into her leg. There was an inexplicable misery in it. She had the dread white swelling. After each swelling the leg perished. Before, when this ache came, she had called Doctor Rollins. He gave her a puncture of chloroform with a hypodermic. Even this hadn't helped in the last few days.

She was glad the Squire was hunting Buck. At home he fumed and swore, spitting ambeer wherever his steps had led him when his mouth filled up, ignoring the fact that she had asked him to spit in the middle of the floor so she could scour it up.

When he first heard of Birdie's condition, he had taken a drink of corn and called her to him.

"I'll whomper hell outen you in more ways than a farmer kin go to town, you lowborned heifer!" he stormed.

Birdie knew he would do it. She wasn't afraid. Since she was big enough, she had fought back at him. Millie was used to these knock-down-drag-out fights. Squire Kiler had used a piece of rawhide on

Birdie ever since she was a little girl, Millie begging for him to stop, not daring to go near him.

He beat her and tried to get her to name the man. When she refused, he beat her again. He seemed to enjoy lashing down on her shoulders with the heavy strap.

She finally gave up and told on Buck. Squire Kiler swore he would kill Buck and old Man Henley Humphries. He'd kill them and burn their house over them. But killing Buck wouldn't keep the child from being born. He thought of marriage as the best way out for him. "I 'low hit's the only damb way I'll ever git shut of her," he told Millie. It would relieve him of responsibility. She had been a burden to him; he had lived in the hope that someone would marry her and take her off his hands. He didn't mince words. He said it to crowds at the store.

His decision quieted him. "I'll go git Preacher Lazenby and then find Buck. We'll come back here fer the weddin'," he told Birdie. She said nothing.

Squire Kiler knew there was black blood in his veins. Millie knew it. She dared never throw it up to him. No man dared say anything to the Squire of his negro blood. He hated negroes. He let them work his bottom place because he said the swamps were the place for pan'ters, possums and niggers. He had ridden horseback twenty-five miles to help lynch a negro in Meedon County. He never enjoyed himself more than when he got drunk and shot up negro meetings. To keep his bottom negroes at home after dark, he spread the story of a strange swamp animal: the willapus-wallapus, which wouldn't eat anything but negroes.

It was he who put the sign over the Forked Deer River bridge at the Neeley-Meedon line:

NIGER DONE LET NO SON SET ON U THIS SIDE

He was proud of this piece of work. He said, "Hain't no tater-eatin', rabbit-chasin', barbed-wire jumpin' son-of-bitch gonna settle down nigh me."

Negroes didn't settle in the Nation. They came in to work for white folks but never let darkness find them there.

Millie was glad the Squire was out after Buck. She didn't know Buck. She had heard he was an awful nice boy but queer-like. She didn't know whether he was the father of Birdie's unborn child. Birdie hadn't fooled her one scrimption. She had known for over two years how Birdie slipped out at night. She hadn't told the Squire. She couldn't endure seeing the child beaten like she was a mule. She said nothing to her daughter. For years she had, through her love for the girl, feared the worst for her. Millie knew she was prime lucky to have but one child. Her first baby was born prematurely and died before the doctor could get to her. She remembered nothing much of what took place as she lay between life and death. Squire Kiler's words meant little to her for days. The doctor had asked Heber, "Where's it at?" "Hit's dead," the Squire said. "Where the body at?" "Hit warn't no count, Doc. Just a little ole wrinkled thing. I takened hit and throwed hit over in the hog-pen."

But it had been a relief when Birdie was born. Then with despair Millie had watched the child grow into an animal like Heber Kiler. With her love for the child arose fear of her. Birdie was something placed in her life as a curse. She inspired no love in her mother's heart, although Millie held on to her, held to the love which she had had in the beginning. "She's mine," she'd tell herself time and time again. "She's all I got. She's mine blood and bone." Yet, there was Heber Kiler's blood in the girl's veins: it had left an indelible imprint upon her. She was more of Heber than Millie—this boisterous girl who folks said had more winning ways to make a body hate her than anybody they had ever seen.

Underneath it all, despite the cursings which Birdie gave her, there still remained love in Millie's heart; as if she were desperately trying to hold on to the only thing which she thought might care for her.

She yearned for someone in whom to confide. She had thought Birdie would be this when she grew up. She couldn't reach Birdie. When she felt she must talk over her troubles with someone, she sought out Aunt Lize Gates. No one but the old negro woman had had a kind word to offer. She listened to Millie and nodded her head in what was enough sympathy for the heartsore woman. After these talks Millie was in a way relieved. Of Birdie, Aunt Lize had said, "She straighten out, Miss Millie. A gal has to split roun' foh she comes into her mind and takes her a man. She's a-needin' of a stiddy man." She would shake her head, its white wool in coiled plaits. "When de moon's in de black hit miseries over folks. Dey hast to keep dey spirits curtained up an' wait foh de full shine. Den ever'thing straightens hitself out."

Millie wanted Birdie to marry Buck and be respectful. Once away from the Squire, a change might come over the girl. Things might work out for the best. Buck would be kind to her and make her a good husband.

Birdie watched the work-worn hands as they shelled the peas. She had never taken time to think of the hands, or the owner of the hands. She was not thinking of them now. She never helped her mother with the housework. Her father forced her to help on the farm. When he was away, she took things easy.

She was thinking of how Squire Kiler had whipped her into telling on Buck. His name had been the easiest to say. Other names would have been dangerous to mention.

She, too, was glad he was away from the house. She had time to think, to make plans. She wouldn't marry Buck. She'd die first. She'd thought of killing her father, of slipping up to his bed while he lay snoring drunk and running her razor across his throat. With him out of the way, she would be free. She was afraid of being jailed for life.

She thought of how she started out. "I didn't have no chance and guess after I once begun didn't want none. I was my ole pap built over and couldn't be nothin' else. We was cut outta the same pattern. I've heerd him say that when I was borned they broke the mold. He knowed he was low and figgered I couldn't be nothin' but him borned over. Somebody tole him a stream cain't rise no higher than its source."

For the first time in years her thoughts went back to the day when she met Bode Holley. She was fourteen then. Pictured in her mind was the long blackberry-lined fence, she with a pail on her arm. She remembered her fright when she saw the weasly Bode. He had been drinking.

Memory stung her now. "I just stood there too skeered to fight. After it was over, I was afeered to say anything. I knowed ole pap would nigh kill me. I hated myself for days. I had to keep it to myself. I thought of shootin' Bode, but guess I couldn't git up the nerve. I guess it was in my blood, but I was takened advantage of.

"Something come over me after that. I didn't keer how I done. I figgered I was ruint anyways. I just turned loose and let folks talk. I didn't keer how I looked or done or whether folks liked me or not. When I laid out of school with two boys, the perfesser expelled me. Old pap beat me blue and takened me back to school. The perfesser was afeered to not let me in."

She thought of the Sobby churchyard and the gang of boys there in the moonlight.

"I shouldn't of named Buck to him, but I knowed it'd cause less hell-raisin'. It'd start him on his way after Buck and I'd have peace to figger what to do. I don't love Buck none at all. He's too queer. And he's too durned young. He never says nothin'. I know he's skeered of me. I led him into it like Bode done me. I durned nigh raped that scutter. He ain't got enough go in him. I want life and a hellacious lot of it."

Birdie liked to be out with the boys at pinchins: Saturday cream suppers and square dances. (Parties were called "pinchins" by the old people because boys and girls got off in corners and pinched and punched at each other "in the most scandalous manner.") She gloried in the weird scream of the fiddle and the nasal voice of the man who called the figures. She liked it when he cried out, "Loosen up the belly-bands and tighten up the traces," for then the party was getting right. She liked to sit out courting under the trees while a visiting preacher stormed at a perspiring crowd; or at Big Singings when faraway music broke sadly against the hillsides.

She studied over all of this now. When she thought of these places, the image of one man came to her; although he had never been out in public with her. Always memory of places was connected with him despite this. It was the man she loved and was dying to see. For months she had known the fierce growing passion for him. She had slipped away to his house in dead of night, to his house where he lived alone. His coarse power overwhelmed her. In his gruff presence she was a weak child. With him she was not the careless, boisterous, don't-care Birdie. Her love made her tender and longing, quieted her.

Closely she had guarded the secret of him, fighting through hungry hours the unconquerable strength of her desire; burning, being consumed by the thought of the times she had been with him. She was drawn powerless to this man. With him she cared for nothing else.

While her father hunted Buck, Birdie sat thinking of the man she loved, of the man to whom she must go. She knew the child was not Buck's. It belonged to the one she loved. In its movements was the power of him. The warmth of it was the warmth of him.

From the first, when lying awake at night after dates which were some way dissatisfying, she had yearned for and dreamed of a man who would be to her the only one. He was this. She had sat here in the kitchen with her mother for over an hour making up her mind to tell: to clean up the whole tangling business and declare herself. She had opened her mouth, the lips full and drooping in their unrest. She had pulled it tightly over her teeth without speaking.

Her mother spoke, her voice weak, timid; as if she feared any minute something would happen, something which she hoped to avoid.

"I 'low he orght to be back soon. Heber generally finds what he goes after. He shore musta got wet as a soaked yearlin' out all last night. Hit's seven o'clock now. I got to go right soon and hep lay out Dossie

Bell Holder. I sent a runner over early to let Luster
know I'd come. I bin mad enough all mornin' with
this here ole white-swellin' to top the high cotton."

She stood now, her hands held out before her as
if they wanted to be doing some kind of work. She
wasn't mad: it was hard for her ever to be mad. She
was a little woman and stooping. Her yellowish-
gray hair was slicked back and knotted tightly at the
crown. Her eyes watered continually. She knew she
had cooked them out over a hot stove. Already dull
brown cataracts were edging into the pupils. She'd
been putting off to cure them like Scudder Tuttle had
his. He'd boiled down red peppers to a thick broth,
drained out the seeds and washed the eyeballs good
with the remaining soup. It burned but was a sure
cure. She was waiting for the cataracts to get ripe
before she tried the remedy.

Her white cotton waist was pinned tightly as the
neck with a safety-pin. Her blue serge skirt bulged
pendulously at her stomach and swung low to the
floor, uneven. She wore a man's plow shoes without
stockings.

"Hit's sech a pitty Dossie Bell laid 'em aside so
younglike. I 'low she warn't no thirty year ole." Still
she seemed talking to avoid a bad impending situation, to keep the gloom air stirred with words.

Birdie never looked at her mother. She wasn't listening to what she said: she wasn't interested in it.
Little things couldn't bother her while she was being
eaten into by big things. Her mind was on the man

whom she loved so savagely. She longed again to be
in his strong arms, to feel the rough stubble of his
face against her breasts, to hear the hard intake of
his breath. She had decided the course she would
take, must take. Her mind was soundly made up.
She would go to him without further delay, before
her father returned.

Mrs. Kiler sighed. "I 'low they'll have the buryin' this evenin' up to Sobby. Hit'll take time gittin'
the coffin and all out from Melburg. Reckon you'll
be a-goin', Bird?"

Birdie sat as if no words had been spoken to her.
She had given Dossie Bell's death a scant thought.
She'd said something like, " 'y God, Luster'll hafta git
him up another woman now that Dossie Bell's quit,"
when she heard it. Birdie never had known much of
Dossie Bell except that she was Luster's woman. She
remembered hearing a lot of talk over how she lived
with Luster. Luster wasn't a bad man for any woman
to love. The big hillman, he of the Cherokee blood,
was cold and noncommunicative, but he was a man
any woman could get crazy over. He reminded her
of her own man in many ways: her man, the least
thought of whom sent new life tingling through her.

"He daid he'd git Brother Lazenby," Mrs. Kiler
went on, "and come out here for the weddin'."

"My cow! I wish you'd shut yore durn ole trap
about Buck and them." Birdie broke out of her
thought in a snarl, dark eyes flashing. "That damn-
fool preacher ain't gonna marry me to nobody." She

slurred each word; thinking, "Me settin' here flusterated to death over my own troubles and her pesticatin' the devil outen me."

Millie said faintly, distractedly, "Hit's sinful to talk agin a man of God, Bird. Hit shore is, now."

"Man of God, me hind foot! He'd be ruttin' round worse'n pap if he wasn't such a ole dried-up woman. He's just the south end of a northbound mule."

Mrs. Kiler sniffed nervously. "I thought you liked to hear him preach and all, Bird. I shore did."

"I went cause it's right nice to be seen in church with yore clothes and all and to see other folks." She raised her voice, high, defiant. "And I went for other reasons which ain't nobody's business but mine. Put that 'ere in yore pip and smoke it! I ain't carin' to cover up nothin' now."

Millie tried to be doing something at the kitchen table. She hadn't wished to get Birdie started. There was no way of stopping her once she began. The longer she talked, the lower the language she used.

"And I'll tell you another thing for it gits cold. I ain't gonna marry no Buck Humphries nor nobody else, 'y doggies. You kin tell my sorry ole pap the same thing."

"Hursh, Bird—" The bent little woman spoke delicately in a rather dead voice, as if she didn't actually want the words to leave her mouth and be heard.

"I ain't hurshin' nothin'. I know all about him. He runs after nigger women, and he's got brats chasin' round half-naked down on his bottom farm. I'll kill him if he ever touches me again. Wy don't you close you durn cutout and let me alone?"

Birdie stood now, one knee bent and extended. As she talked she shifted to the other knee, her hip sticking out roundly.

She cleared her throat and spat hissingly between her front teeth. "You all made me lie on Buck. This here," she said bitterly, pressing her stomach, "This here ain't none of Buck's. I know whose it is and I'm goin' to him. They ain't no use tryin' to stop me. It's takened me a long time to figger what to do, but now I know." She clenched her hand tightly. Her face was a steaming red, the red of her neck disappearing beneath her loose dress.

Mrs. Kiler regarded her daughter, her pale watering eyes filled with fear. She didn't ask questions. The words choked in her throat. Something told her she couldn't stand the shock of hearing. There had been too many shocks of late. She stood as if fettered to one spot on the floor, her body trembling. Listlessly she wound her hands in her skirt, not knowing what to do.

Birdie had calmed down. "I got my things packed in pap's ole valise," she said. "I'll inform you sweetly, I'm leavin' this here place for good and all."

Millie Kiler didn't hear these last words. She never watched Birdie leave. What reason she could command told her something dreadful, more dreadful than could be imagined, had happened; more dreadful things were to happen. She wished out of all of it so she might never know. Something from the outside, unseeable, seemed to fall over her narrow shoulders like a black shawl: an intangible, encompassing net which smothered her body, her senses.

She sat down and looked at nothing. She sat for minutes, thinking of nothing. She came to herself and tried to probe back into the time-blank through which she had just passed. She wished to find a peace she had never known.

She left the house and walked into the woodlot adjoining. She continues to walk, her dimming eyesight melting out objects as she approached them. She hadn't noticed she could barely see things at a distance.

She reached the big road and climbed a rail fence. The effort made her heart beat rapidly. She had to rest before going on. She stopped at the spring and washed her eyes, trying to believe afterward she was seeing better.

She hadn't known where she was going at first. She thought of Dossie Bell and set out in a wavering path for Luster's cabin, the image of death trailing after her. She struggled up the hills. It would take some while to get there.

She hurried too much for one with a fluttery heart. She had to get to Luster's. She wanted her hands to be at work, her mind occupied with other things.

The woods frightened the failing woman. She had heard tales of the lonely hills which led to Luster's cabin.

She imagined strange things and saw strange things through her filmy eyes: *A green glazed wind walked rapidly past her. Above her head blood-foaming panthers skimmed through the branches like a procession of water-spiders. The Shadow of Death scurried at her side. Opal-eyed blood-foaming panthers continued to follow her, fastidiously, delicately, through the oily hickory leaves; sinuously, undulating, through the tangle of wildgrape vines.*

12

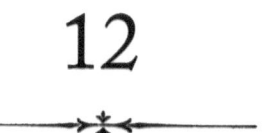

LUSTER AWOKE and looked about him. Sunlight danced through lacy cedar limbs and played in shadows on the floor. He had slept in the rocking-chair like a dead man. His neck was stiff. He worked and twisted it with his hands to loosen it up. He wondered why he hadn't gone to bed right.

All returned to him slowly. Dossie Bell lay on the bed cold in death. Sudie Lazenby sat opposite him, sleeping as quietly as a child. She had been asleep when he returned from nigger Pud's creek hut. Luster hadn't troubled to undress. He had kindled a little fire and sat down to dry his clothes.

He had thought quickly on awaking, "I'll go into the kitchen and warsh up. Dossie Bell she'll have breakfast on the table—sowbelly fried in meal, what some folks calls Rocky Mounting trout. She'll say, 'The coffee's hot, Luster. Ere you ready?'"

He'd thought all this before the sticky sleep film was gone out of his eyes. Now, he relived the past night. The death of his woman was something far off, unreal.

It was late in the morning. The rain had ceased.

He never woke Sudie. "I 'low she's tard. Other folks'll be over soon. The bad night hit's kept them home."

He washed his face and put on a clean blue shirt. He combed his straight black hair. He was still combing it when he heard a scratching at the door. He opened it. Tommyjohn, Dossie Bell's cat, walked in, her flossy tail high in the air, her entire body shaken by vibrating purrs. She rubbed against Luster's legs, tilting and pushing her head this way and that.

He picked her up. Unconsciously he stroked her fur. His 32-20 S & W lay on a marble-topped bureau in the corner. He spun the cylinder, saw it was loaded, and stuck it in a side pocket of his overalls. He took a milk-bucket from the cook-table and with Tommyjohn under his arm, walked to the barn. He found Balky and milked the bucket to overflowing with warm foaming milk. Tommyjohn meowed and meowed, waiting hungrily. Luster poured a panful of milk for the cat and stooped to watch her while she lapped it up, her red tongue clipping in and out of it. When she finished, Luster left the barn, carrying her with him.

He stopped at the pond.

He sat the milk-pail down and found a stone. He took a piece of cord from his pocket and tied one end to the stone. He tied the other end around Tommyjohn's neck. Tommyjohn continued to purr electrically.

Luster raised cat and stone above his head and tossed them far out over the middle of the pond. Tommyjohn fought the air for a minute, too late realizing danger, hit the water and sank in a circling ripple with one water-choked squawl. The stone pulled her to the bottom.

Luster picked up the milk-bucket and paused longer to watch the ripples on the muddy pond gathering and gliding bankward to disappear. He looked to the east to see shaggy moth-eaten clouds lying soft against a dove-blue sky.

He heard a wagon rattle back toward the cabin. Harve Buckner was helping Urfie Pearl, Clemmie Bean and Granny Blackburn to the ground. They had finally arrived to see Dossie Bell and help lay her out. They would cook a big meal's vittles, ask a lot of questions and gather a passle of news. Sudie could talk to them. They'd dress Dossie Bell and get her ready for the burying up at Sobby.

Luster set the pail down and crossed the pasture to the creek. He waded into the rushing muddy water to reach the edging of woods. On the sandy bank he stopped to listen. A kingfisher swooped along the water. He heard a stirring among the bushes.

Something whisked through the air above his head and hit a beech behind him. He examined the tree. A railroad tap was embedded in the bark.

"Come out, Wurner," he called sharply.

The stocky man peeped at Luster through a sparkling green covering of wild-cherry leaves, his little eyes blunt and turtleish. He pushed his head out. His short low-ground teeth were in a spreading grin. He waddled toward the tall hillman.

"Hit's Mister Luster now. You was Mister Luster. I don't know then. I think a burly cow. I shoot zing, zing, fastlike and hard. I come out to see you. I come out from down Low Mud Creek. What do you'uns think of that?"

"What you wantin', Wurner?"

"I seen him way back. I seen them right away short off."

"Seen who?" Luster looked down on the squatty Wurner Crouse and waited, unhurried.

"That preacher-man yistiddy. I seen him goin'. I seen him goin' from yore kitchen. He was goin'. I went up there and went in there. She was gone way off. You was gone way off. He was goin'."

He stood, legs sprangled-out. Clayey sand rose in small wiggling worms between his toes as his broad feet sank into the oozy creek bank. His overalls were rolled halfway up his bulging hairy calves.

Luster lay a hand on his shoulder. He gazed steadily at the blank red face, the twisting grinning lips.

"Brother Lazenby was out here yistiddy?"

Wurner nodded. "I seen the preacher-man way back. I seen them right away." His leaden, wandering eyes, filled with dumb worship, shifted over Luster's tall form.

"Who right away?" Luster asked patiently.

The idiot pointed a stubby finger.

"They's down yonder hid. Mules with black and white man. They's hid and snake it now nigh Indian mound. What do you'uns think of that?"

"They're snakin' out a log?"

Again Wurner nodded his massive, shaggy dark head.

"You go to the cabin, Wurner. The women folks'll give you something t'eat. Help Pud with the coffin if he gits back fore I do."

Wurner laughed hackingly. "I eat a lot to yore cabing. The coffing hain't came." He waddled into the creek and off in the direction of the cabin.

Luster entered the woods and walked along a sunken logging road which was overgrown with high yellow-flowered weeds and thick seeding grass. He climbed to a ridge and stopped to listen. There was no sound but the hissing wind. He removed his shoes. He selected a slender pine and skinned up to the lower limbs. He pulled his body high among the topmost needles. The breeze swung him from side to side.

His eyes swept the country for miles. They settled on a spot in the Dinney Hollows. He could see the green top of the Indian mound above the branches of giant red-oaks.

Back on the ground he set out in a curving path.

He walked for over an hour before he again halted. Through the underbrush he could see four gray mules. They were hitched to the butt of a red-oak trunk. The tree had been recently felled and trimmed. Two negroes and a white man were in an argument. Behind them the mound rose high.

Luster stopped and waited.

"I say," the white man spoke angrily, "we better haul our tails outen here now and not wait. We kin come back whilst he's at the buryin'. We kin leave the mules back of the mound. Nobody won't find them." He was a stranger to Luster. He was thin, his chest sunken. His face was swarthy, the stubby mustache like something which didn't belong to it. He wore an old army coat and shoddy blue trousers.

"Hit was yo idea comin' las' night, Mister Glatham. You sho picked one mo' hell of a time. You knows I'se afeered of sto'ms."

"I knowed hit was a good time, Lobe. The minute I heerd his woman was dead, I seen a chanst to git another tree. I didn't have no idear the storm'ud come on us."

"Who a-think he'd send Pud foh dat coffin? I was sho he'd go hissef. I ain' gonna fool myself up agin dat Indian." Lobe was a tall black whose shoulders spread in a slope to send his arms almost to his knees. He wore a pair of jeans without a shirt.

"You don't know Luster Holder. All he's study-in' now is gittin' her planted and roundin' hissef up another hussy for winter."

"You let him heah you say dat and you'll be fur-nishin' a new tombstone foh folks to read off on Sundays."

"I'se ready to git dis heah out now." The other negro, a round-stomached fat buck, talked complain-ingly. "Us kin move hit fast 'case he's up to de cabin gittin' things ready."

Glatham whirled on him. "Who tole you to open yore goddambed loose trap, Frogeye. Yo're in a fair way to git yore guts cut out."

"I does a little carvin' on de side mysef."

"Ain't hit de truf!" Lobe said. He and Forgeye had their hands in their pockets.

Easily Luster worked from the bushes. He was almost up to them before they saw him.

The three stood stock still, slouched. Their hands and arms seemed in their way. They looked from Luster to the mules and back. No word was spo-ken as Luster's eyes moved from one to the other, recollecting.

The fat negro, Frogeye, broke from the group. He ran suddenly and rapidly toward the mound, yelling "I'se done sold out of dis settin'."

The report was quick, deafening. Frogeye reached high, seemingly trying to grab his hands full of air. He went forward on his face, legs working spasmodically; as if, although dead, he were still fleeing from danger.

Wide eyes settled on the smoking 32-20 in Luster's hand.

Lobe plopped to his knees, begging. "Foh de Lawd's sake, white man!"

Glatham licked his lips, measuring the distance to Luster. He sprang, shrieking, "You goddambed halfbreed bastard!" His knife was open in his hand.

His lank body hurtled against Luster's knees. Luster fell to the leaves, throwing his body into a spin. The knife ripped through his jumper sleeve, as Glatham worked desperately to reach his throat. Lobe hadn't moved, although he held his razor out and opened.

Luster's right hand caught Glatham's in a twisting grip. The knife dropped.

The gun was against Glatham's chest. "Please, for Jesus Christes'—"

Two shots, close together, cut off his words. Lobe's big eyes were round and white. He dropped the razor. He looked as if he wanted to run but had lost control of his body.

He stood shaking like a wet dog as Luster walked toward him.

"Gimme a chance, Mister Luster. I'll do anything foh you. Hones' to God I will!"

Luster raised the gun and struck Lobe between the eyes with the barrel. The big negro fell flat on his back, moaning and twisting. The white of his eyes had changed to red.

The hillman looked down on him, studying. He put the gun in a trouser pocket.

He drew back a heavy shoe and kicked Lobe hard in the ribs.

"Git up."

Lobe rose cautiously, holding his head.

"Put them bodies on top of the mound. Then take them mules up to my pasture."

"Sho, Mister Luster, sho. I'll do anything." Lobe's expression was of a man who didn't believe he was actually alive.

"When yo're through, git to hell offen my land and don't let me never see you agin."

"I sho won't, Mister Luster. I sho as God won't."

Luster glared at the black distastefully.

"Git on." He ripped his jumper sleeve and looked at his bleeding arm. The knife had cut through the skin in a curving gash.

The negro had shouldered Glatham's body and was struggling up the steep mound, pulling to limbs and bushes.

Luster saw someone come from behind the mound and slowly advance toward him. He saw the torn khaki hunting-coat, the muddy boots. He recognized Buck Humphries.

The boy's face was white despite the coating of brown, a sickish white.

"It's Buck," he called thinly.

Something in the worried young face, the matted curly brown hair and startled eyes sent the hillman's mind back, puzzled him.

"I saw them," Buck said breathlessly. "I was afeered. I was a coward not to help you."

"I wasn't needin' no help."

"You was wonderful."

"Where's the Square at? You knowed he's huntin' you?"

Buck talked fast. "I dodged him all I could. I come on yore land. I thought he wouldn't find me here. I'm tard out. I cain't go on no longer. I'm nearly starved. I'm sick and afeered." He hid his face in his arms. "I ain't gonna marry her. I cain't!"

Luster rubbed his arm. It was getting a little sore.

"I'm afeered, Mister Luster," the boy blubbered. "I'm a coward, but I cain't help it. I want to see Dossie Bell."

The muscles of Luster's face tightened, then relaxed. Lobe was halfway up the mound with Frogeye's pudgy body.

"You go crost the creek to Aunt Lize Gate's cabin," he said, indifferently. "Tell her I sent you. Stay there till this here blows over. She'll feed and bed you."

Buck lifted his head. His cheeks were stained in dirty streaks. "I'll go. I cain't know how to thank you."

Luster turned toward the ridge.

13

Back and forth through the entangling jungle of underbrush Luke Tolby and Bode Holley stalked each other. Since the first somber light of early morning the two men had searched for an advantage. Tolby knew Bode would get out of the hills and slush into swamps impenetrable to the average man. Bode was a born swamp-rat. In the bottom country he had a chance to shoot it out with the eagle-eyed Tolby. Luke held no fear of Bode, but Bode was dangerous—sneakingly dangerous—in this territory.

The giant Tolby man moved cautiously through the canebrakes and waited with a patience peculiar to all Tolbys before him.

Luke's grandfather had settled in western Neeley County way back when the land was uncleared. Artie Tolby built a big double-walled log house in the mountainlike red-clay hills. He set out ten cedars in an even row before the door and said, "No man kin pass under them cedars alive lessen I says he kin." He and his six sons kept outlanders from settling in their part of the hills.

Artie and his sons robbed and killed. In the Nation, it was said, some folks were killed and others just found dead. They buried gold in iron washkettles at marked spots over their land. They defied all law and order.

On the house walls, Artie kept a record of his killings:

Jun 8, 1854. Got me a Cantrell

Dec 10, 1857. Paid ole Cole Beard. Blowed his head off

Owe Murl Pierce a det. Got him mar 1, 1858. He was lowratin us Tolbys roun

Feby 18, 1875. Got plugged in leg but boared ole Pete Sims twixt the eyes

Luke recalled the story of Artie's death. The old man's daughter, Jimmie Lee, had been nursing her baby in the big-room with her father. Artie got up and went outdoors. After an hour, Jimmie Lee called to Mertie Bob, her youngest sister, who was in the stove-room cooking:

"Have you saw anything of pappy right previously?"

Mertie said, "Pappy he must be dead. I ain't heerd him cussin'."

He lay, in the backyard, dead.

His final request that his body be stacked high on logs and burned by the neighborhood boys was carried out. Great crimson flames intermingled with angry rolls of black smoke "to carry me on to my folks in Hell."

Thought Luke as he stalked Bode Holley: "How kin I be the grandson of sich a man and be afeered? Specially of a skunk like Bode Holley. Cain't no man steal none of my licker and lowrate no lies on me.

"I'll blow his head right offen his shoulders. I'll leave him just like he's a dead cow or hawg or anything I'd hauled off to the bottom. I'll leave him to rot, for the buzzards to eat offen. Hit'll be a warnin' to any man which wants to cross up a Tolby.

"I've got to git this over with right quick and go up to Dossie Bell's buryin' at Sobby. Luster I don't suppose would give a damn either way. Cain't nobody tell what that man's thinkin' no time. Hit gives me the jinkers to be roun' him. His folks run mine outen the Nation, but what else could they do but leave out with them wild men after them a-burnin' and a-killin'. I'd shore like to have them lands back. I'd hafta do away with Luster. I'd hafta plan hit keerful. I'd hafta shore do hit secret. When you mess with a man like him you shore better have yore brain wide open.

"I'd like to know whur or not Squar Kiler's foun' Buck. I'll feel better when Birdie's married to that 'ere boy. I 'low the Squar kin find him if anybody kin."

Bode Holley squatted behind a water-oak. His face was puffy from drink. He squatted forward, froglike, his narrow shoulders slumped, his white-knuckled hands holding a Marlin 30-30. He could see the heavy form of Luke Tolby not twenty yards away. He raised his gun, furtively, trying to steady it in trembling hands, overanxious.

"I could kill him, I believe, but I hain't shore. It would be just too bad, Isham, if I missed. I've saw Luke drop squirrels with them skinnin' round a hick-ory fast as striped-tailed apes. If I could shoot as good as Luster Holder, I'd try from here. Luster could bust his pipe right outen his durn filthy mouth."

All through the day before, Bode had stayed in his cabin with Ludie. He had sat apprehensively watch-ing the cabin window and taking frequent drinks to steady himself. Ludie had begged him to be careful. Luke Tolby might be out in the bushes waiting. She was all torn up with anxiety. He longed for night so he could make it to the woods.

Through the hanging afternoon he had sat and kept his eyes on the window, the blinding sunlight dulling to his spirits. He had time to think of how foolish he was to steal Luke's keg of whisky and sell it out on the streets of Melburg. He had helped with the run and known where it was buried. Ludie warned him. Then he got drunk and told lies on Luke at the Firbank store.

He had time to think of Luke Tolby, the dark, brooding, humorless Luke Tolby. He would feel weak and have to take another drink, his woman begging him not to get whisky-brave.

Night had come on slowly and with it a fretful wind. Clouds, like smeared pokeberries, hid the lowering sun. With darkness was silence. The ravine where the cabin stood was wiped out. Ludie said it was mizzling rain, that he could soon leave the house in safety.

They had both been scared white by a knock at the door. Then with the "Hullo!" they were eased.

Wurner came in, his long muscular arms clasped behind him. On his face was an expression of bewilderment. In one hand he held his slingshot.

Bode stared angrily at the idiot. "What the hell you mean skeerin' me?" he demanded.

Wurner shook his massive head ponderously without speaking.

"You big Christian fool," Bode said, "I'm a mine to bore you though the guts."

Wuner clasped and unclasped his stubby hands.

"Them talks agin God shall—them shall burn up, clean up. What do you'uns think of that?" He smacked a hand flat against the house wall.

Bode hadn't wished to get Wurner mad.

"What you wantin', Wurner? Hurry up! I got troubles mysef."

The stocky man waved his hand aimlessly.

"Miss Dossie Bell she'd dead now. I went by there and she'd dead now all right. I'm tellin' folks. Luster he's went off." After these words he left.

Ludie begged Bode to watch out. He left her, tearful in her uneasiness. He skulked away to the low country.

Luke moved into a canebrake and Bode lowered his gun. He shook his head and knew a dizziness. Moisture popped out on his forehead and worked into his eyes. He had drunk a half-gallon of licker during the night. His head was throbbing: it was a throb like the pierce of a knife—the complete throb fulling, heavy—then the interval of cessation which came to make the next throb more pronounced.

His mouth was dry as birchbark. The tongue had separated from the rest of the mouth. He lolled it around, feeling he'd like to spit it out. "I'd like to find that man," he said aloud thinking of an old joke.

"I'll vomick in a minute," he reasoned.

He took a drink from a quart bottle. "Jesus-God! but this here's rotten," he talked-out again, clearing his throat hard, hawking and spitting; for the moment forgetting the nearness of Luke Tolby. "You kin feel the verdigris runnin' round slickin' up yore stummick. You kin smell the gag. I shore wish I had a tracer."

He sang to himself, low, whiny, nasal:

> "They laid her in a coffin made of red;
> They put a lace cap on her head.
> And they said that she was dead;
>   And they said that she was dead;
>   And they said that she was dead."

14

Birdie took a shortcut across the fields. She sank to her ankles in the low places, sandy soil overlapping and partly filling her shoes. She crossed a pasture dotted with chalky rock, crawfish holes and the yellow blossoms of prickly-pear and waded waist-high through a patch of broomsedge to reach the creek. Slim leopard frogs, gold-green and lavender, slipped through the rough grass as she passed. Furred spiders with folded legs swayed gently on their webs above her head as she parted the willows. The shaggy bark of wildgrape vines scraped her ankles; briars and scrub thorns tore at her bare legs. The air was pungent with the smell of moist leaves.

In her mind was the thought of him to whom she was hastening, distance alone holding her from him. Her father, Buck Humphries, the child, were forgotten. Thought began and ended with her lover.

She hadn't told her mother his name. He had cautioned her against this. It would mean death. She didn't care. Without him she wished for death. It would take death to keep her from him.

A sharp breeze off wet vegetation cooled her cheeks. She felt alive and free for the first time in days. And like something wild and akin to earth she moved, aware of the fulness of youth, the sinuousness of her brown body.

She crossed Cleeburn Creek, wading through, her skirts held high to her hips, her refelction dancing zigzag and rippling away before her in fading distortion. The wooded hills hung around her and crawled back in great lapping folds of trembling pine and crisp, dark oak. She climbed the last ridge and approached the squat cabin. Crossing a horse-lot, she entered the kitchen without knocking. She hurried through the empty rooms. She threw her valise under Tolby's bed.

Luke was not at home.

She glanced over the room, her lips drooped in disappointment.

"He's gone to Luster Holder's, I'll bet my bottom dollar," she said to herself.

She lay across his bed, tangling the dirty quilts about her thighs. She was aware of a feeling of contentment through her unrest. "I love this place more'n life," she whispered again and again.

From the back doorway she saw through feverish eyes the hills receding until they reached the bottomlands. The sun was passing through thinning clouds: clouds wispy, ragged like the underbreast of a white hen. "The clouds is troublin' the sun," she thought absently. "It'll be a day of light and shade."

Densely in varicolored green, trees walled in the river. She could see the break where it ran. Buzzards floated aimlessly in and out of sight. Bluish vapor melted rapidly as sunlight sifted through it.

A gun sounded, hollow and dismal, far down toward the Forked Deer. It was a boom, then dead silence.

The sound disturbed her; yet she thought of Luke. He was near. She would soon be with him.

It was Luke for sure, she figured. He had gone hunting. She knew he wouldn't go any place where there were dead folks. He was scared of the dead. Superstitious-like. She fingered the hawk's foot suspended from a string at her neck. It kept evil things away.

The gun sounded again. Luke was hunting Bode Holley. That drunken old coward Bode Holley. She sure hoped he shot hell out of him. Luke would fix him so he wouldn't be spouting off at the store. Couldn't anybody fool Luke for long.

"I'm goin' to him," she said in a raised voice, chanting. "I'm goin' to him, the gun it's a-callin' me. I'm goin' to him, the gun it's a-callin' me."

She forgot the heaviness of her condition and ran hurriedly across the horse-lot, her soft breasts escaping from beneath her low-necked dress. She pushed through a windbreak of locust trees. She was exhausted by the time she entered the bottomland. Swamp-grass wet her dress high up and tickled her legs. Mosquitoes and gnats circled her head, biting her neck and arms. She struck viciously at a devil's-horse which aimed its long nose at her and swooped past her ear.

She stopped short, her mouth gaping open. A long gray-black snake moved sluggishly into a slough. It lifted its head, its wicked little eyes set dead upon her, and darted its tongue in and out rapidly. The still green slime parted and cleaved back as the slough swallowed up the crawling body.

Birdie paused for moments, eyes stretched. A chill swept her body.

"It's a cottonmouth," her mind warned her. It'll kill you if it bites. Nothin' but strong licker'll cure the bite."

She recalled hearing her pap say that the cotton-mouth and the regular water-moccasin had bred-up together to make a more poisonous snake. She called, "Luke!" and heard the words echo from the fastness of cypress and water-oak. She thought of the time a cotton-mouth had bitten Louenie Kimm. Louenie had swelled double her size and spots as purple as pokeberries had come out on her. Her folks wrapped her up in a plaster made of blue creek mud mixed with a stew of jimsonweed and yellow percoon root. She'd laid in bed a long time before getting back like to common.

Recovering her nerve Birdie walked under vine-hung trees; and, not knowing just which way to go, headed in toward the river. Every little while she stopped, cupped her hands around her mouth, and called, "Luke!"

Finally he answered, his voice cracking out to her left. She circled a canebrake and, following the sound of his hulloing, found him squatted by a log, his gun between his legs. A week's growth of beard darkened his heavy jowls. Tobacco-juice drizzled from the corners of his mouth. His corduroy suit was slick yellow, his greasy hat pulled low on his forehead; his boots wet and clay-caked. A quart jar of red whisky sparkled on a stump near him. He'd just been saying to himself before she came up, "I'll have one more little snort to stiddy me." He knew it was double-run, charred corn. It would hold a bead the size of Number 5 shot. There were no rabbit eyes on it to pop off like fresh, watered-whisky did.

His mud-brown eyes showed dull and stupid on seeing the girl. He got to his feet, puzzled. He sensed his danger.

"Hursh!" he hissed. "Bode he's down here. He's after me and I'm after him. We bin stalkin' each other fer hours. I've fared off my gun twicet to try and skeer him out. He's afeered to show hissef. We got to keep quiet. He shorely heerd me holler." He

stopped and peered hard at her, as if she were someone he'd never seen before. "What the hell you follerin' me down here for?" he demanded coldly.

Her eyes were on him widely, burningly. She
breathed fast. Now that she was with him, she sensed
her body weaken. With him she was always weak:
a quiet girl far different from the Birdie Kiler folks
at Firbank knew.

Her words were faint, hardly above a whisper.

"Honey, I had to see you. I've come to you."

"Did which?"

"I've come to you. I couldn't stay away no longer."

"You know damn well you *hain't left home?*" He
drew his brows together in a hard frown.

Her head was lowered, her hands clasped. "I
couldn't help it. They was goin' to make me marry
Buck Humphries."

He drew closer to her.

"I love you, Luke. I got to have you," she said
huskily.

He shook her roughly, his hard hands like nails
biting into her shoulders. Whisky fumes were strong
on his breath.

"You comin' down here when I got other troubles!
I tole you to stay away from me! I tole you we'uns'ud
hafta keep this thing quiet! Now you've named hit
to them and ruint us both."

She looked into his dull eyes, eyes bleared from
overdrinking. Her olive skin was hot with throbbing

blood. Her mouth was still open, her full lips wet and quivering. Her hair curled into her eyes.

"I ain't told them your name. I love you. I had to find you." Her desperate tones rose from low in her throat.

His grizzly face was almost against hers. Veins like greasy red rivers interlined his eyeballs.

"I hain't havin' no more of you now or no time, 'y God! Put that 'ere under yore belt and buckle hit down!"

"It's yore baby, Luke. It's yo'rn and mine." A feeling of misery assailed her.

"Hit ain't none of mine, you runnin' after ever' man in Neeley County! You'll git back home and marry Buck Humphries!"

She shook her head. "I cain't. I won't," she said hoarsely, decidedly. She didn't raise her voice.

"You won't skip hit. You've ruint my life, me tryin' to do right by ever'body. Now I got to take out fer Missouri or some'rs or nother till this here blows over."

She threw her arms around him, pressing herself hard against him. She held up her open mouth, striving to reach his. He tore away from her and knocked her down, his heavy fist crashing solidly on her cheek.

She lay quietly, not crying. Blood ran from her mouth in pinkish foam. She lay quietly in the dark decaying leaves watching him with wide childish eyes, staring, eating eyes.

He prodded her with his foot. "Git up and git gone! I hain't gonna be bushwhackered by no Bode Holley just because of you!"

She watched him, the man she desired and couldn't have, her eyes still longingly sinking into him.

He scowled down on her, not certain what to do next; thinking, "She's my sister's child, the daughter of old Squire Kiler, whose grandpaw was a buck nigger. I was a idiot to ever fool with her. She's purty as hell. There was something about her which tuck me in. I seen her grow up and seen how wild she was gittin'. When she come to my cabin, I just went crazy over her. I didn't have no idear she'd git to lovin' me with all them young fellers hangin' round. I broke her in and now she's follerin' me. I cain't git shut of her. I orght to of killed her fore this here ever come up."

She lay like a wounded animal. Her eyes were swimming black to him. Her face faded in and out in distortion. His head was dizzy. He had drunk too much. He beat his fists against his temples. If he got too drunk, he knew Bode would have the advantage of him.

With one hand he jerked her to her feet. Her arms encircled him again. He tried to shake her loose. He cursed her. She pressed her open lips over his, drawing against them. In their struggle, they fell to the ground. Luke's head struck the edge of the stump. He lay still, she clasped to him. She stayed for minutes with her face against the matlike hair of his chest.

She sat up and looked at him. He was unconscious. "He's nigh drunk too," she reasoned.

She sat motionless by him looking down on his dark face. Terrible thoughts came to her, thoughts of everything being finished for her.

"He won't have me. I'm lost now. He won't have none of me no more. He's through. I'm left with nothing. He set me afar and left me to burn up. They ain't gonna be no more bein' with him and knowin' his strength, lovin' and lovin'. Ever'thing's blowed up. But ain't nobody else gonna have him, I soundly know.

"I'll do it while he's out. I aimed to do it if he wouldn't have me. I thought hard on it for days and grew afeered. But I finally made up my mind to do it if he wouldn't have none of me."

Her razor was open in her hand. It glinted mirrorlike as a ray of the sun broke like a spear of gold through the canopy of leaves and vines.

She hadn't thought it could be done so easily. She found herself enjoying the doing of it. Blood darkened the blue of his shirt and ran sluggishly through the hairs of his chest.

She was relieved. No other woman could ever have him. He was dropped from her life, but she could live on nursing his memory.

She sat for a long time thinking of him as he had once been. She kept running a smeared hand through his tangled hair. She kissed his paling lips.

"I guess Bode Holley ain't needin' to see you now, honey," she said tenderly. She laughed unnaturally, despairingly. "Yo're dead and don't know it. I'm kissin' you and you cain't help yoreself."

A gray spider crawled onto Luke's face; carefully it stretched its legs as if measuring each step. She made no attempt to knock it off. She leaned over and cleaned the razor on wet moss.

The quiet of the woods startled her. She began to realize what she'd done. They would lynch her. She didn't care what happened just so she wasn't lynched. She didn't want a crowd watching her die.

She would have to hide the body, put it where nobody would ever find it.

15

SQUIRE KILER LED THE WAY into Luster's cabin with Brother Lazenby close behind. The minister was nearing a state of collapse. His naturally sallow face was red and swollen; his eyes puffed by insect bites. His seersucker suit was drawn-up and stiff with mud, the trousers torn at one knee. He dragged his feet and breathed heavily.

He scarcely noticed where he was going. The Squire's broad back guided him, he following as if drawn by some gross power. He felt irresolubly bound to Kiler's will.

Earlier in the night he would have welcomed the sight of any cabin. Now he didn't care. He had lost all signs of fright and seemed resigned to anything. The big Squire was a demon in human form; there was no natural blood in his veins. He looked as fresh as he had before they left on the meaningless search for Buck. He was forming new plans to find the Humphries boy. He seemed not at all putout by the result of the night. He acted as if he thought the time well spent.

Brother Lazenby knew he meant nothing to Kiler. He hadn't been taken along because he could be of any use: he was dragged into it because the Squire had never liked him and wished to wear him down, wished to show him a life of which he knew nothing at all. He was carried along like a whip by this old man who loved trouble and lived for it.

In the death-room they found Sudie Lazenby. She was where Luster had left her, her yellow-green eyes distanced away. The door to the kitchen was closed. The rattle of stove vessels and dishes mixed with a constant chatter of conversation came muffled through the panels.

"Whur's Luster at?" demanded the Squire. He threw himself into a chair and spat a cud of tobacco into the dying ashes. Brother Lazenby lay down on the floor and pillowed his head on one arm.

Sudie paid them no heed, seeming unaware anyone had entered the room. She was as silent as the dead hill-woman.

"Dashburn hit!" the Squire growled impatiently. "Cain't nobody talk? Whur's Luster at?"

Sudie's face was in a set stare. Her lips moved. She wet them and began talking.

"I couldn't help it." Her voice was lifeless, hollow. "I couldn't. I had to come out here after I saw him. I sat here and I couldn't keep my eyes off him. I thought, 'I can't ever escape him and I don't want to.' I must have been somebody else that wasn't me. That somebody did it, and that damns me. All the Christian I was disappeared last night."

The preacher was sound asleep. Squire Kiler smoothed on his thick eyebrows and scowled straight at the talking woman, puzzled.

"Done whut?" he asked, out of temper. "Has yore mind went out on you?"

Her words were tender, wistful. "He drew me to him like a child to the fire. I forgot all about my God. Someway my God left me. I saw only those gray eyes. I sat there watching them, and a power in them got into me. I became filled with that power. When he came in and called me, I went with him. I was scared, but I had to go. I lay there on a pallet in the kitchen and his big brown body was next to mine. I forgot everything else." Her fingers, long and graceful, trembled in her lap. She appeared to be talking to no one.

The Squire spat in disgust. His thick eyebrows beetled angrily. "Hit whoops me. Hit sho-God whoops me. For Ole Billy's sake, whut's this here preacher's wife a-babblin' about?"

"Then all which had been me came back suddenly," Sudie continued monotonously, singsong. "I lay in there after he'd gone and saw my old life finished. I said to myself, 'I can't pray it out. I'm changed beyond redemption. I'm changed and it's too late, for I can't regret it.' I find something beautiful in thinking of it."

Squire Kiler's face was livid. He didn't say anything more. He chewed a fresh piece of tobacco, working his jaws back and forth doggedly. Brother Lazenby snored, groaning and twisting.

"I turned myself loose for the first time. I did just what I wanted to. I knew it was a sin but all enjoyment is sin. Me coming to believe this damns me eternally. I know I'm not what I was, for there is no regret in my heart."

Kiler eyed the snoring preacher. He prodded him in the side with his foot. Brother Lazenby turned over and breathed easily. The Squire walked to Sudie and shook her. He glared into her dazed face, her set eyes.

She came from her state of trance. She fully realized the presence of others. Meekly she raised her face to the Squire. Blood tinted her hollow cheeks.

"I gave myself up to Luster Holder last night," she said in a low soft voice. "It was on a pallet in the kitchen. I sat here thinking and thinking; while he watched me, never saying a word. When he called to me, I went with him. I can never forget him."

The Squire sneered. "You come and takened advantage of Dossie Bell. You done hit. Wy don't you keep hit to yoresef? Hain't nobody keerin' none. We got our own troubles to see after. 'Ere you tryin' to git the preacher het up? If yo're wantin' him to still breathe God's free air, you better keep Luster Holder offen him."

Sudie appeared not to hear. "I gave myself up to him. I can't think of anything but last night. I saw Urfie Buckner and them others come in this morning. I never moved. I didn't want to do anything but sit and relive what had passed. They'll tell everybody. They're in there now whisperin' over it. They'll turn me out at Sobby like we all did that poor woman over in the corner. But I'm beyond caring now."

Squire Kiler blew out his breath sputteringly between his thick lips. "You a-shootin' off yore mouth and yore man on the floor so tard he cain't hear none of hit," he said scornfully. "Hain't nobody keerin' a damn whut you done. You orght to be proud to of laid with a man like Luster Holder. I cain't blame you after knowin' whut you bin tied-up to."

Again he prodded Brother Lazenby with a heavy boot. With a sigh of infinite weariness the minister sat up and looked around him drowsily.

"Git up, preacher. We got to start humpin' hit if we git Dossie Bell planted this evenin'. Hit does look like some more of the damb curious 'ud be here by now to hep out. I wonder what the glorious hell's a-keepin' Millie? 'y God, hit's funny Luster hain't in too, and not much funny neither. He sholy hain't went out to make no run this mornin'. I wouldn't put hit past him though."

Brother Lazenby stood up.

A flat silence held the room. Watery green light glowed from the hickory shade outside the window. Faint yellow sunbeams quivered on the floor.

The Squire pulled stiff hairs from his ears. He spoke in a sober voice. "Hit beat's Jesus the troubles I'm havin'. Buryin's and preganant daughters and hidin'-out bastards. Me raisin' her right and all. I knowed I was throwin' mysef away when I married into that 'ere low-flunged Tolby fambly. I'll find Buck Humphries if hit takes a hundred year."

Brother Lazenby stooped to the floor and busied himself by scraping mud from his shoes with a pocket-knife. Through the torn gap of his trousers, his knee-cap stuck up like a piece of white marble. Sudie kept her face to the mantel. A hum of conversation drifted in from the kitchen.

No one knew when Luster entered. The big hill-man moved noiselessly. He glanced about him with the certain look of aloneness peculiar to him. Seeing the grouping of folk, he stopped, seeming not to believe their actual presence. It was as if he thought the room to be always bare of humanity since Dossie Bell's going away.

With his entrance the room seemed filled with animation, the strength of his body diffused over everything. Yet, there was about him something intangible, shadowy.

He sat down by the south window.

"Have you sent for the coffin, Luster?" Squire Kiler asked, yawning. He noticed Luster's torn sleeve, the stains.

Not taking his eyes from the window, Luster said with indifference, "Nigger Pud's went to Melburg after hit. I 'lowed Dossie Bell'ud like gray better'n most colors."

"Gray's sho purty."

Luster turned to the minister. "The buryin's to Sobby at two this evenin'."

The kitchen door opened. Granny Blackburn stood fanning her apron. Her wrinkled face was red from stove heat. Her head shook from side to side uncontrollably. Stringy hair escaped from her black bonnet. She drew her toothless mouth in and out as she chewed. Her bare feet and stilty legs were a blotched purple. Behind her Urfie Pearl Buckner and Clemmie Bean bent over the stove. Wurner Crouse sat at the cook-table eating.

"Luster," Granny Blackburn said, "that goddurned stovewood's so green hit wouldn't burn in hell with a blower on hit. We'll never git the vittles cooked." She spat a gob of snuff which spread octopus-shaped on the floor.

"Hit must-a rained on hit last night."

Granny's glazy eyes stayed on Sudie Lazenby.

"We've did our best to git you'uns up a mess of grub. But I hope to roast out my miseries with the devil, if Wurner don't shovel hit down as fast as we git hit cooked. He sets thar grinnin' like a dog eatin'

sand and snortin' into hit like a durn brood-sow.
You couldn't pull him 'way from that 'ere table with
a team of young mules. 'y God, he could eat a bull
and hit bellerin'."

Squire Kiler yawned.

"I figger you better git home and clean up, preacher," he said, rising. "I got to be gittin' on myself,
Luster. Thar'll be others in soon. They's enough
here to lay her out. Damb if I kin know what's holdin' Millie up. I'll be to Sobby for the buryin'."

He left the room. Brother Lazenby followed
him.

Granny Blackburn returned to the kitchen.

Sudie kept her eyes from Luster. He seemed
unaware of her.

16

IN THE ROTTING LEAVES by Luke's side, Birdie forced herself to study and study what to do with the stiffening body. One hand, flaked with drying blood, lay carelessly in Luke's coarse sunburned hair.

She couldn't recall the living Luke. This dead body was nothing which had ever been the Luke she had known. It was now a worry, something to hide away for protection of self. Her love, too, was forgotten with Luke's going. It had disappeared with him. Memory was connected with death. Fear remained, dumb fear.

The doing of the murder had been easy; the thinking of the doing, the realization of the deed, spread over her until she sat like a little child who has suddenly broken a cherished toy, the useless pieces scattered about her.

She attempted to brave herself by talking. "He's dead," she kept explaining. "And I done it. All that's him now is breathin' in me. He's went some'rs else. He wouldn't have me, so I sent him off nowheres that's knowed of."

Then she would try to play tricks on her actual knowing and pretend. "He's just asleep. He'll git up after while and put them big arms round me and hold me so clost I cain't git no air." She knew no strengthening at the weird idea.

Birdie had thought before today that nothing could ever separate them: God, man, nor the devil. Up in his cabin with him it was hard to think otherwise. She herself had brought the final separation. He would have no more of her. She had to wipe him out.

Now thoughts of her own safety outweighed thoughts of the gone Luke. She experienced no grief, only fear of discovery and increasing hate for all which had brought her to ruin.

"They'll lynch me for this. They'll git men and hounddogs and hunt me down. My ole pappy'll help them, cause they ain't nothin' he likes more'n a good lynchin'. They'll run a loop of rope over my head and pull me up to a limb. They'll yell and cuss and shoot a lot of lead into my body. They won't think of the baby. They'll kill it too."

A feeling of smallness, helplessness, pervaded her. She fought this off in the dread of things to happen.

She had to hide the corpse. The river was the best place, but she couldn't drag it that far. She cast about for another place. She saw a group of young holly trees, their leaves growing low and bunchy to the ground. She got to her knees. She was stiff and sore. The weight of the burden pulled her groundward.

She took Luke by one leaden arm and tried to move him. She tugged hard, only rocking his long heavy frame. She tried to drag him by the hair.

"He weighs a ton if he weighs a ounce," she gasped. "He's cheatin' me even now. He's dead, but he's still cheatin' me."

She fell across the body and breathed shortly. She got up at once, for the first time in fear of the dead man. She began piling leaves over him. She wished to get him out of her sight as soon as possible. She scooped up big handfuls of decayed leaves and poured them over his face. She rested and poured more.

She knew she'd never get him covered up this way. She needed a shovel or hayfork.

She heard the sound: distant, now nearer: a hoarse song falling through the entangled mass of vegetation. Soberly she made out the words:

"Oh, I was borned in Arkansas,
  And I never knowed my paw;
  I just growed up with swamps and rattlesnakes.

"I lived a decent life
  Till I met my neighbor's wife;
  I stayed at her house while he was way."

Stupidly Birdie listened, not wishing to bring herself to the thinking of who it was.

"I thought all was runnin' right
Till he caught me there one night;
An' that's why I left ole Arkansas."

"It's Bode!" she cried to the dead man. "He wouldn't be singin' if he wasn't drunk. He's licker-brave. He's comin' this-a-way!" She was wide awake to danger; thinking, "He'll find out I done the killin'."

She scooped more leaves over the body. She hadn't quite covered the face.

"Oh, they fired anvils when I run away;
Oh, they fired anvils when I run away;
Oh, he fired anvils when I run away;
Cause women hain't safe nowheres that I stay."

Birdie didn't see the bushes part behind her and the man peer out from a cave of leaves. She didn't wish to see. She knew he was there. She could hear him, almost imagine she smelled the whisky he was drinking: this was enough to hold her suspended in increasing dread.

Bode stepped out and swayed above her. She saw his leather boots, wet and shiny, specked with clinging trash. She knew it was Bode Holley. She rose slowly and brushed her hands tightly against her dress, standing guiltily. She twisted her neck and looked at him, all of him. One side of her face was swollen, bruised black where Luke had hit her. "I must make out I ain't skeered," she was telling herself. "I must keep hold of myself."

Bode Holley was very drunk. He was hatless, his cornsilk-colored hair damp and pasted in sweaty strips on his forehead. The yellow stubble of his face was dirt-smeared. In one hand, swinging carelessly, its barrel muddy, was a Marlin 30-30.

He stood weaving and pitching, trying to concentrate his gaze on the girl by closing one eye. He lopped his tongue across his salmon-pink lips. His skin was waxy: it looked as if it might break through his cheek-bones. His overalls hung loosely on his weasly body.

"Hit's that damn Tolby," he said thickly, leering hard at the corpse. "You done killed him. Me huntin' and huntin' fer him and you done already killed him. Cheated me outta doin' hit." Even in his groggy state he experienced great relief at seeing Tolby dead. With Tolby gone he was brave.

Birdie's mouth was open and round. A nausea spread over her while she strove to face him calmly.

"I ain't done it, Bode Holley. I found him here. It's you was gunnin' for him. It's you shot him," she said weakly, a note of futility in her recrimination.

Bode laughed raucously. "Hit look like he done shot with a razor."

Her body was out of control. "It's you done it. It's you done it," she repeated mechanically. "You shot him in the back. You was afeereder than hell of him." She tried to talk firmly, but her lips quivered.

"Think you kin dam'lie me cause I'm drunk, eh? They hain't no use denyin', Bird. I hain't tellin' on you. Glad the son of bitch's gone."

He attempted to walk to Birdie. He circled wide and fell flat on his face. He raised on one elbow, leaves sticking to his chin.

"Tha's all righ', Bird. Glad the bastar's dead."

"I love him more'n life," she mumbled absently.

Bode jerked his head back sharply to throw hair out of his eyes.

"I hain't surprised," he said. "Hit's a wonder you hadn't bin lovin' that 'ere sorry old pappy of yo'rn."

He sat up. "You wasn't barrin' nobody. And then you tried to stack hit off on a puny little boy like Buck Humphries."

He set his eyes greedily upon her, taking in the sinuous lines of her body where her wet dress stuck to her. "She's a beaut even if she is swole outa shape," he thought.

"Yo're a purty heifer, Bird," he said. "You was made for me. I'm wantin' a new woman. Me'n Lude's through."

She continued to glare down at him. "God," she thought, "I've shore reached the jumpin'-off place. Bode Holley's lower than ere nigger. Him tryin' to kill a man like Luke. Luke might be livin' now but for Bode Holley. I hoped I'd never see him agin."

Her eyes filled with loathing, hate.

He saw the quart of whisky on the stump. He crawled over and unscrewed the lid. "This here'll be the first and last thing Luke Tolby ever give me. The old peckerwood did make good drinkin'-licker. I'll just have a puff to sober me up." He tilted the Mason-jar to his lips and drank long and deep. "Good God from Gulfport, but this here's fine. Hit'd make a man burn his own barn."

Almost instantly he straightened up. The liquor cleared his head a little. He clambered to his feet and staggered to where Birdie was standing. He held the jar out to her. She backed from him.

"Look-a-here, Bird," he said seriously, new ideas coming to his belickered mind, "what you need's a little drink. Yore nerves is shot. This cuttin' th'oats an' all has sorter fizzled you down. Take a swaller and you'll be settin' jake."

She pushed the jar away, her eyes on him sullenly.

"I ain't takin' nothin' from you now or no time, Bode Holley."

His face hardened. He leered at her through pale-lashed slitted eyes.

"Who misformed you on that?"

"I ain't takin' it," she said despairingly. "You out drunk killin' my man."

He caught her by the throat with one grimy hand. She fought, scratching and biting. He forced her head back. He pressed on her jaws to open her mouth. He held her rigidly, the jar to her lips. He poured her mouth full of the yellow fluid and held her until she swallowed. She sputtered, choked, her stomach regurgitating. The whisky ran onto the front of her dress, cooling her breasts, penetrating to her stomach. He let her catch her breath and poured her mouth full again. This time she swallowed most of it. He threw her from him, cursing.

"I guess a little drink'll remine you who done the killin'," he growled.

She gasped, gagged, tried to vomit; but the spirits warmed her insides, entered her veins. Her entire body tingled. She felt better, of a sudden strong. She was more Birdie Kiler now.

"Feel better?" he asked.

"I shore-God do."

"I knowed you would."

"I want another hum in a minute."

"Let that-un git organized and we'll both take one. I don't want you to vomick on me. We got to throw Luke in the river."

"Will you reelly help me, Bode?"

"Yo're durn tootin' I will, Bird. Hain't nobody never gonna know who done hit."

Her eyes, wide and shining darkly, opaque, studied Bode somberly. There was no dullness in them now. She frowned at him speculatively. Her lips were compressed with a certain sinister determination. This determination made her stronger every minute.

Bode wasn't looking at her. He fingered the quart and appeared to be figuring out something in his groggy mind.

They drank together, slapping and punching at each other, laughing loud echoing laughs. He was aware of the exuding heat from her young body through the thin dress. He pressed her breasts with rough, eager hands. He tried to kiss her. She pushed him away.

"We got to hide the body." She cast an oblique glance at him.

He grinned. "We shore have, now." He studied a minute. "We'uns had a good time oncet, Bird."

"Yes," she said flatly. "Yes, we did oncet." Talking as if her mind were far off from the river-bottom.

On through the thickness of vines and bushes they pulled the heavy body of the dead Luke Tolby. Briars and thorns tore and scratched the pallid face.

At times they had to stop and rest. Birdie falling panting to the ground.

Then on toward the river.

They reached the willow-grown banks of the Forked Deer. The wet slime-covered remains of the tall Luke Tolby was slid down the slanting bank. It paused at the bottom of the bank, suspended for a moment, doubled, head between outspread legs. Bode pressed his boot against the drooping head and shoved hard. Without a sound the corpse was taken in, consumed and swept away by the rain-swelled current.

Bode sat down and held his head in his hands, shoulders swaying.

He's passed out, Birdie thought, as she saw Bode reel over into the stiff crabgrass and lie still. She bit her lips and the new feeling of strength came back to her. A strange smile exposed her even teeth. Her eyes were wider and darker, unmoving. She stared straight at him, then over him as though at something terrible, fascinating.

She walked toward him.

17

THE HILL ROSE HIGH over the surrounding ridges. Slanting downward from it, in gradual rolls, the oak-and-pine-covered land receded to a creek which crept snake-fashion through a deep ravine. The land rose again to melt away skyward into dim blue haze. Toward the east, far away, lost in a density of trees, lay Melburg, the county seat of Neeley; smoke from the stave-mill there blurred into the foam of snowy clouds hanging above it.

On this highest hill was the Sobby church-house, a single-roomed white frame bulding whose shingles were rotting and falling off, ruffled and torn by the blustering storms of many Marches and Aprils. Squat on its wood-block pillars it stood lonely and isolated in the heart of the Nation country. The cleared ground around it was hard cracked clay, beaten and

packed by generations of hillmen; by mules and horses; buggies, wagons and old-model cars.

Back of the church was the Sobby graveyard.
Cedar trees marked head and foot of most of the
graves. Long lacy-green limbs swept low to the
mounds. The wind soughed through their bunchy
limbs with a distant quiet.

The oldest tombs were blackened with age, their
names and dates unreadable. They told of what
the person died—bronchial pneumonia, smallpox,
typhoid fever, membranous croup; and the maker's
name was carved in large letters in one corner, his
address given. On each of the tombs, underneath the
name of the deceased, was a little verse:

He has gone to live with Jesus; his earthly life is stilled;
A place is vacant in our home which can never more be
*   filled.*

I was a professor for fifty years.
Now I've gone to reap my reward in Heaven.

Listen, stranger, as you pass by.
As you are, so once was I;
As I am, so will you be,
So follow Christ and come with me.

She was a little flower
Budded on earth to bloom in Heaven.

At home there is an empty chair
Which drives us all to grim despair;
We pray to God in Heaven above
Because we know our loved one's there.

She lived the life that God loves best;
She kept the faith; she stood the test.
Now she's nestled on her Saviour's breast
At home in Heaven forevermore.

Far from the awful cares of earth a little angel will sing;
The beauty of her love for Him did all His blessings bring.

Oh, we loved him; yes, we loved him.
But the angels loved him more;
And now they've sweetly called him,
To God's own Eternal Shore.

He believed, he trusted, while others mocked;
Now in God's cradle he's gently rocked.

Little Brother's laughter we hear no more;
Too soon from us he's taken.
His little feet tread the Golden Shore;
In Heaven he did waken.

Crudely carved boards marked many of the graves, the names and dates written in pencil. Over several were straddled chicken-coop wooden structures to keep the rain off; sometimes these protections were built of sheet tin. Always was the hillman's horror of having rain or snow fall on the dead. Decorations of broken crockery and mussel-shells strewed the mounds, were sunk into the clay by wet weather. Faded artificial flowers stuck out of Mason-jars.

Far down in one corner of the graveyard, edging into the thick bordering of pine, oak and hickory, three men, two white and one black, shoveled out a new grave; piled the rich red earth high to one side to find a last resting-place for Dossie Bell Holder.

The sun was breaking through racing clouds. The air was humid, heavy, pressing-in. The blue shirts of the digging men darkened with sweat.

"Dat rain sho didn't soak down fah," the negro said from low in the deepening hole. He worked in his undershirt. Greasy beads of sweat collected on the shining ebony of his forehead. His big yellow bullfrog eyeballs protruded from their sockets. "Dis here groun's hard as a railroad-arn fah a fac'."

"When you 'low the buryin'll take place, Gert?" one of the white men asked the other.

"Hit ain't gonna be no year off, Arnie. Folks is already drivin' onto the churchgrounds. Hit's about two now."

"They say Dossie Bell Holder was a awful good woman."

"She shore was, now. She always looked like a purty woman looks on Sunday morning. She never married Luster, but they was happy just the same."

The negro paused to map his face with a blue bandanna handkerchief. "Mister Luster he sho a straight-up man. He mean when he git stahted. But he sho never botherates nobody lessen dey sets him off fust. He say foh us to git a good grave dig. He gwine pay us a gallon a-piece. He ain' axin' no man to do nothin' free."

"Some'un was a-sayin' the Square hadn't found Buck Humphries. I always tole my woman no good'ud come of no boy which solitared roun' like Buck done. Nobody never knowed who his mommey was, but they was strange tales tole on her anyhow."

"Buck's crazy, Arnie. He shore is. Nobody never accused Birdie Kiler of bein' nothin', but I figger she's in her rights now."

"Buck and his ole man orght to be run outen Neeley, Gert."

"Hit's the sarned truth. And when the time comes, Arnie, I'll be right on hand with my passle of guns."

"Yo're durn tootin'. I'll stand by, myself, and see a lot of meanness did, but I ain't gonna watch no man dessicrate no young gal without doin' right by her."

"Me and you too, Arnie. When he seen she was in trouble, he dropped her like a hot wedge."

"Dey says Mister Luke Tolby done out gunnin' for Mister Bode Holley. Dey's gwine be a scrubbin' out dere one way ot t'other."

"I 'low hit'll be Bode gits bumped. He's skeered to death of Luke. That 'ere Tolby's a mean shot, now."

"He's had more fights than anybody in Neeley County or anywheres else, 'y God. His whole fambly was bushwhackers. They kept folks outen their part of the country for years. He's the last of the Tolby menfolks."

"I figger he'll be breathin' roun' here a long spell yit. When Bode gits the best of Luke, the jaybirds'ull be singin', 'Who'd a-thought hit?'"

"They say Luster Holder's the only man he ain't never messed with. Hit's bin lowrated he's afeered to cross Luster."

"You'd be, too, if you'd had Luster lay you out cole as a winter punkin."

"He didn't, now?"

"He didn't skip hit."

"How's that, Gert? I wonder why I never heerd? That musta bin when I was workin' in Deetroit, Mitchigan."

"I disremember the exact time. Hit was kinder hurshed down. Folks was afeered to tell hit out here and hit didn't make no difference out there. Hain't nobody from out there ever comes out here, kinder stayin' to theirselves. Hit was over to a strawberry supper in the Meedon settlement. And you know how bad them bullies is. Pole Meedon and his ole man was both there with far-arms showin'. Most folks was skeered to go. But Luster and Luke they went along. Luster he taken Dossie Bell and his 32-20. Luke he takened a razor and pair of knucks.

"Luke he got too much corn and tried to make up to Dossie Bell. Hit takened five men to git Luster unclamped from his throat."

"He called him by the name, did he?"

"He reelly persuaded him, I mean!"

The negro grinned, his mouth sparkling full of broad horselike teeth. "Mister Luster sho ain' afeered on nobody."

"When Luster crows, day reelly breaks, I solidly inform you without no stutterin'. He'll do them wood thieves the same old how when he ketches them. He's a stem-winder shore."

Gert climbed out of the grave. "I 'low this here's deep enough to cover a dead hoss, let alone a woman. Pud," he said to the negro, "straighten off the corners a little. We'uns don't want to leave no grave whomper-jawed. Me'n Arnie'll go down to the spring and warsh-up for the buryin'."

"Yassah, Mister Gert."

"You stick roun' to hep cover her up. And git a stob trimmed to mark the grave."

"Yassah, sho, Mister Gert." He paused, his eyes big with expectation. "Gimme one of dem tight-rolls, please, sah." Gert fumbled a package of cigarettes from his pocket, worked one out, and handed it to the negro.

Dossie Bell's funeral was well knowrated over the hill country. In continuous streams people drove over the winding, climbing roads from all directions. They came in mule-drawn wagons, extra spring-seats and canebottomed chairs filled with men, women and children, of all ages and sizes, dressed for the funeral. Yellow hounddogs and mingled breeds of black-and-tan, brown-and-white spotted dogs came with them, trailing behind or walking in front of the mules or foraging in the thick Johnson- and sedge-grass along the road-banks. There were horse-drawn buggies with colts whinnying near their mothers; other buggies with courting couples, who made their horses go slow, linger. Hillmen and their boys, horse- or mule-back, clopped along, appearing and disappearing as the hills lifted and dropped them. Model-T Fords, overflowing with large families, bumped and choked.

From Sweet Lips and Harmony; Pinetop and Robey; Pilgrim's Beauty and Snakey Ridge; Violet Blue and Land of Joy; Frog Jump and Lizzard Lick; Panther Branch and Turkey Bend; Possum Trot and Bear Hollow; the Kinney Flats and Scudder's Mill— they came to overflow the little church-house until many had to swing in the windows to see.

Coming on and on, more and more, they hitched and climbed out. Women straightened and pulled down stiffly starched cotton dresses or wrinkled and faded silk ones. They worked over their children's clothes with a fussy sort of tenderness. They took their children far into the scrub oak before entering the church. Men and boys gathered in groups to chew and smoke, to talk over every little and big thing with like interest.

Squire Kiler, Brother Lazenby and Sudie arrived together in the Squire's green Weber wagon. The Squire wore the same muddy clothes in which he had hunted Buck Humphries; still unshaven, he was more gray and scowling than ever. Brother Lazenby wore a blue serge suit, and a celluloid collar with a black bow tie. He was fresh-shaved, his face powdered, pale, his small eyes still red. Sudie's black silk dress tipped the grass. A bow of green ribbon circled her waist tightly. Her crushed black hat left her hair-club high up and out behind.

"They's seats perserved up front fer friends of the fambly. The church-house hit's full." Squire Kiler bit off a piece of plug-tobacco and ground it onto his jaw-teeth. His gray eyes narrowed. "I sho cain't figger what's went with Millie and Birdie. They wasn't nowhars about the house."

Sudie didn't speak. With head lowered she entered the stuffy church.

"Brother Holder hasn't arrived with the remains. We can't get started until he comes." Brother Lazenby took off his gray felt hat and held it in his hands.

Squire Kiler scratched a hand whistlingly across his corduroyed buttocks. "He'll git here 'fore long. He's bin busy as a cat on a tin roof. Tole me he'd hafta wait to granny a cow which was calfin'. Looks like they hain't no end to his troubles. An' hit's a hellacious drive frum here to Luster's cabin. He hast to cross two fields and the creek to reach the main road. His wagon-tars hain't no good noway. I got to set nigh the back of the house, preacher. I takened a dost of medicine 'fore I left home to regulate me up some."

Brother Lazenby frowned. "I'd like to be through with it."

"I 'low you'd be sorter tuckered out after last night. Do you have yore sermont ready, preacher?"

Brother Lazenby looked away. "I'm not sure, Brother Kiler."

"I 'low you better do right by her, preacher. If I was you, I'd not pesticate Luster Holder. Hit's easy to die, preacher. Hit's hard as hell to live."

Cooter and Carnes dragged the squeaking old wagon onto the grounds, Packer and Hobart at their sides. Luster sat on one end of the coffin box, his hardhide shoes pressed against the front board of the wagon. The dull sun brought out the whitening blue of his jumper and overalls. Wurner trailed.

Heads appeared in the windows. Those who jammed the doors whirled to see, pushing and shoving. "Luster and them's come with the corpse, Mommey!" a little boy hollered excitedly. His mother thumped him. "Hursh, Nestor."

The Squire, Luster and Wurner lifted the box from the wagon-bed. They unscrewed the lid and raised the gray casket out and onto the ground. They carried the coffin box out through the high grass, over blackberry, honeysuckle and ground-ivy and placed it by the newly dug grave. Pud sat with his shovel, smoking and waiting.

Wurner stayed with Pud. Luster and the Squire returned; and, one at each end, took the casket into the crowded church, down the center aisle through the hushed assemblage, and set it across a small square table in front of the pulpit. Brother Lazenby walked after them.

Luster sat down on the front bench near Sudie. She held a handkerchief squeezed into a tight ball in one slender hand. Luster unlaced his shoes and pulled them off.

Squire Kiler paused to examine the casket. He saw the gray cotton cloth, the rigid design of it, the nickel-plated handles; the plate on top with AT REST stamped on it.

He took his goose-quill from his mouth.

"Hain't that the purtiest coffin you most ever seed, Luster?"

"Hit is, now," the big hillman answered glumly. "I 'lowed she'd like gray better'n rosewood."

The whole western end of Neeley County and many from other counties had turned out for the funeral. Men and women talked and whispered across the aisles; to those at their sides and behind them. Little circles scattered over the house.

"That hat comes right at you, Doney. What did it set you back?"

"A dollar forty-nine at Forbes'. It's highway robbery, Rhodie."

"Forbes has ground the farmed down for twenty year. He'll reap a hot reward hereafter. No wonder his woman can wear silks and satins."

"They say she has four pair of shoes."

"How can a body use over one pair at a time?"

"Ardie Percy's here with her young'uns. They take up a whole bench. She's a-settin' up straight and stiff in a corset she cain't spit over."

"How many's she got now, Cuffie?"

"The last made fifteen. Her man's so old he's nigh bent double."

"That don't make no difference. A man kin git up a young'un as long as he kin blow a feather off his knee."

"She's back there now dippin' and spittin' like she was on her own front porch. They say she likes snuff so well she eats it. I cain't see for the world how her man keeps that family in dips."

"She told me last time I was out at her house that they all dip snuff 'ceptin' the baby and it takened a little dip now and then. You know what she and her man does when they want to leave the young'uns and go to a dance, cream supper, Big Singin' or anywheres? She told me herself. They spread out pallets on the floor and then give the young'uns a round of licker. When they're all drunk, she and her man goes."

"If I had a face like hers, I'd keep it in a sack till the dark of the moon."

Praise God for truth! She's ugly as homemade sin."

"How's yore chickens, Hexie?"

"My best rooster he has the bumblefoot. He hobbles roun' like he was walkin' on far-coals."

"Melvie Murchison's cow got in Jodey Peake's sorghum patch and foundered itself. It was about all they had except a smile and suspicious looks. Quick, Hexie! Look at Eller Sullens. A bedbug's playin' base round her collar like hit was midwinter time. If I was gonna try to be filthy, I'd git out in the hog-pen and wallow with my kind."

"I don't see Brother Karns here, Odie. He never misses no buryin's."

"No, Hexie, his wife had to flirt out one of his bad decaded teeth last week. He's bin awful sick. The tooth was shore bedded down in the gum. She nigh broke the spoon-handle. The jaw swole up twicet hits nateral size. Matter and carruption flew ever which ways. He had to quit Big Meetin' over to Golbert's Bend."

"I do say it!"

"Penny, Old Miz Beechem's settin' over there happy and fat as a town dog. And don't know where the next meal's vittels'll come from."

"Her man'll steal taps off the railroad and sell for scrap-arn, or roastin' years outta somebody's late patch."

"Obie Taylor lawed him last first Monday for takin' meat from his smokehouse. They's also a bill agin him at Melburg for stealin' the carpet outen the Pilgrim Beauty church-house."

"Dexter, I bin dyin' to talk to you and git some of yore remedies. How does a body cure thrash? Talbert, my youngest, has it."

"Call in a body which ain't never saw its father and git him to blow in Talbert's mouth."

"You mean a body which father died 'fore it was borned?"

"Yeh, a posthumorous child."

"Thank you, Dexter. Now, Steller Buthren said you knowed how to cure earache. My six howls with hit nigh ever night."

"I squeeze the juice outen Betzy bugs in the year. That humbles the pain right where it's at."

"I'll shore do hit, Dexter. And now what about white-swellin'? I'm all pussed-up with hit."

"My own salve cain't be beat. I done the mixtry mysef and'll send you send you a box. I cain't give the receipt out, but I'll tell you the makin's. Hit's tare blanket, yellow percoon root, boneset weed, sarsaparilla, sassafras, Queen of the Meadow, cherry bark and May butter."

"Love and thanks to the grave, Dexter."

"I wonder did Squire Kiler find Buck."

"I hope and pray he did. I was skeered stiff for my boy, Omer, when I heerd it. They'd bin talkin' and sweet-heartin' for some time. I says, 'Ere you gonna git down in the dirt and waller like a durned mule? You stay away from her if you want a roof over yore head.' I throttled him down right short."

"Wy, Clemmie, she's bin splittin' roun' the country lookin' like she'd swallered a watermellon seed and had hit sprout. It looks like she would of had the decency to stay at home."

"I soundly know it, Urfie Pearl. I looked for her to drop it right on the streets of Melburg. She looks hogeous, buckin' here and yon smilin' like a mule eatin' briars, and not wearin' enough clothes to wad no shotgun."

"Wy, mustard-seed! I ain't got no use for Buck or his old pappy neither, but they're good as she is. It hurts me to think how pore Millie Kiler hasta drudge her life out. Pore thing. She shore set down in it when she married him."

"The pore soul's eyes is about gone. And that 'ere white-swellin's plaguin' the very devil outen her. I begged and plead with her to use my linament remedy. It's made outen dirt daubers' nests and vinegar."

"That spread made by boilin' down hogweed and mixin' with tar and taller'll knock anybody's white-swellin'."

"I wonder where Millie's at? I figger though she had to stay at home and watch after Birdie."

"She cain't manage no Birdie. Millie hain't no bigger than a cake of soap after a hard day's washin'."

"That old Square comin' up from his low beginnings and tryin' to be the highcockylorum of this here community! Them Kilers is the rakin's and scrapin's of the earth."

"I don't a grain dispute it. The world's boilin' and the scum's risin', Urfie Pearl."

"It shore-God is, I mean. He should be tuck down a notch or two. I've wanted to say things to him so bad I could taste it. I'd like to tell him to go to hell and tell the devil hit's a hog I've sent him."

"Now yo're shoutin' if you ain't jumpin' up and down!"

"Clemmie, I got to move my seat. That 'ere chucklehead of Nody Heps has ruint hits clouts. I cain't stan' hit no longer."

"I don't know whur the Square'll find Buck or not. I'd hate to go footback through them bottoms after anybody."

"It'll be hell and highwater when he does find him."

"Them's the words with the bark on them!"

"I figger our country's shut of Buck Humphries for good."

"Thank the Lord and bless the cook!"

"I wonder where Luke's at?"

"He's percolatin' roun' some'rs or nother."

"Does Sheriff Blackstock know about the trouble out here?"

"He shore does, 'cause my man named it to him yestiddy. Blackstock won't be moseyin' out in the Nation. He'd rather see his box and it open than to mess round out here. Them laws ain't so dumb."

"Koline, how do you make yore persimmon beer?"

"Well, Lady Bob, I take two gallon of persimmons. Then I let my persimmons sour in water. Then I add a quart of sorghum molasses to my persimmons. I sink a pone of cornbread in it and let stand for seven days. I strain it and let stand for seven more days. I drein off the scum from the top and it's ready to drink."

"I figger I'll haft to add a little licker to it or I know Zeke and Card won't tech it. I'm tryin' to figger how to keep Zeke from stayin' drunk all the time. He's got so he won't take sweetmilk, unless it's teched up with corn. It's set a bad example before Card. Card he ain't but fifteen, you know, but he's come in drunk four time in the last month. Him and his pappy staggers in holdin' each other up every so often."

"Ain't that Card over there with Leslie Pandrey's gal?"

"Yes, look at them settin' half-hammered! I bet he's lit up now. He's bin tomcatin' around every sinst he was knee-high to a tumble-bug. I'm gonna git drunker'n a bitch myself sometime and burn the durn house down on top of him and his old pappy both."

"I never seen nobody diked out like Sister Lazenby." Look at them frills and frizzles on her dress."

"My cow, Whistel, folks well knows Brother Lazenby cain't offord no high-falutin' clothes. Her tryin' to look like a millionaire!"

"A lotta rags a-flyin' in the air! Him with his money in chips and shavin's and her wearin' brought-on clothes!"

"Maybe she's tryin' to look purty for Luster Holder, Luler."

"What kin you mean, Whistel?"

"I guess it ain't no secret by now. Urfie and Clemmie seen her with their own eyesight when they went to set up over Dossie Bell. She'd been there all night with him and nobody else in hollerin' distance. She was settin' asleep in a cheer. She knowed they were there, but never made a hand's turn to help them."

"All night in the same house with a man like Holder?"

"I said it and I didn't stutter. Course, I ain't arguyin' that nothin' went wrong, but the looks of it don't offer no peace of mind."

"She's settin' up there by him now. You noticed how she takened a seat where he'd have plenty room to scrouge in next to her."

"Nothin' else which happens at Firbank ain't gonna surprise me one fiddlin'."

"Wonder who Luster'll git as his woman now Dossie Bell's died on him?"

"I 'low he won't have no trouble a-tall findin' some prideless hussy. It orghtn't to be put up with among decent folks. But Lord knows how to curb down a man like Luster."

"There'd be a passle of women'ud flock to him if he'd give the signal."

"You spit a mouthful, Thible."

"Brother Lazenby he looked skeered at something."

"I figger he ain't got no more notion than a hill of beans what to say, Dossie Bell not bein' a wife and all. Oh, the sins of this day and time shore pulverize a body down to the point of nothin'!"

"You've heerd the stories bein' lowrated about him, how he's bin slippin' out to Luster's to see Dossie Bell?"

"I don't take no stock in them lies. Brother Lazenby is a Christian-man if ever there was one borned."

"Yeh, folks is right ready to frazzle-out a body's reputation if you give them the eighth of a chanst. Him riskin' his life to save her black soul, and folks spreadin' dirt!"

Luster's back ached where the low bench struck it. He watched how Brother Lazenby stood, uncertain, frozen, gaping dazedly at the congregation. He wished the preacher would go on and get it over with. He knew nothing of funerals. His woman's dying had brought him out to his first one. It didn't make any difference what Brother Lazenby said. He knew best, as he was a preacher.

"I 'low he'll say Dossie Bell's lost. I hain't keerin' a damn. What him or them others says cain't hurt her now. I figer she'll git to Heaven if any of them does."

He thought of the new calf at home. "If I hadn't bin there to granny ole Pattie Pide I 'low hit'd be dead now. Pattie Pide shore couldn't have borned hit by herself."

Again he could see how its head had been folded between the forelegs: its glassy marble eyes on him

stupidly; how it swayed, too weak to stand. Pattie Pide
was Dossie Bell's cow. The new calf was Dossie Bell's;
but she'd never see it. She aimed to call it Dimity if
it was a heifer. It was. He would call it Dimity. She
was crazy over Buck. He guessed she would have
liked for Buck to have it.

Brother Lazenby leaned with his elbows against
the pulpit stand, his head lowered. He looked about
him. His whole body was numb and sick, not like his
own. The church was hot and steaming. There was a
strong smell of sweating people. Everything blurred
before the minister's eyes: the waving palmleaf fans,
the solemn human faces.

He couldn't keep his eyes from Luster. The big
hillman's expression was deadening. He seemed to be
waiting for something which he was anxious to do.
His brown feet were pushed back under the bench
as he rested forward, elbows on knees. Sudie, beside
him, had her gaze directed to the floor.

Brother Lazenby looked over the gray casket and
beyond the crowd in the rear door.

"I'm sure he knows everything. I tried to change
my life when I might have known it was too late. I've
got to start a song so I'll have more time to think.
Squire Kiler warned me to be careful what I said. It
don't make any difference now."

He motioned to Elmer Runnels. Elmer, a lank
sharecropper stood with a songbook in one hand

and a tuning-fork in the other. He struck the fork against the top of a bench and sounded his voice, a high thin tenor. He had to strike and sound three times before he found the key.

"Number 206," he announced. "'We Shall Meet on That Golden Shore.'"

The song began low and reached a volume which shook the small church-house.

Little boys and girls chased one another up and down the aisles. Somebody in the center aisle called out, "Calm them tappers down!"

A mother stopped singing to cry shrilly and nasally, "Ocker Lee Sealey, I'll beat the paste outen you when I git you home! Just wait and see if I don't!" She hit out at him with an advertisement fan—a give-away from a Melburg store: the picture on it, in browns and reds, was of a young boy and girl in riding-habits, each holding a jar of snuff.

"Come here, Pistol." A man jerked his little boy to him roughly. "If you don't shut up, I'll churn you!"

A woman slapped her baby hard to hush its crying. "Lisern here, that 'ere sniffin's got to be curbed down." She reached far into her waist, searchingly, and pulled out a breast for him. "Want yore jug, Puddin-Pie?" she asked gently. He sat wobbling on her lap, eyes tear-filled and wandering, impatiently fumbling with rosy hands.

A child choked on the cracker it was munching. Its mother beat it in the back. "It's went down yore Sunday pipe, Madie."

Other women had brought pacifiers for their babies: little bags of sugar—sugar-teats. Some of the larger children were eating candy-and-crackers.

The song gave Brother Lazenby time to think of fearsome things. One question pounded in his brain, chilling him: Did Luster Holder know? Yet, what difference did it make now? There was nothing to look forward to, little to live for.

The whole terrible scene returned to him. He remembered the smallest details of it:

Crouched in the willows, he pushed the foliage aside so he could get a clear view of Luster's cabin. He watched the bare clay yard, the kitchen door. For more than an hour he had been watching, waiting, debating with himself the possibility of the hill-man's absence. Twice, with an impatience brought on by nervous tension, he started from his hiding-place and out toward the pasture. Each time some inner caution stayed him. He breathed easier when he saw Luster emerge from the kitchen and head for the south woods. Dossie Bell lingered in the doorway to see him leave.

Bent low, Brother Lazenby traversed the pasture and mule-lot and hurried up the steps to the kitchen. He stood by the cook-stove, breathing fast, trying to regain his composure before he faced her.

"Sister Holder," he called timidly.

She walked into the room slowly, showing no surprise at seeing him. She was a small woman, delicately formed. Her brown eyes, overlarge, were fringed by long curving lashes. Her mouth was pale-red, girlish. She hadn't done up her gold-brown hair. It sprayed over her narrow shoulders and halfway down to her waist. She wore a gray-checked gingham dress, black stockings and slippers.

"Hit's Brother Lazenby," she said in a clear voice.

The minister picked at the frayed edges of his coat-sleeves. "Where's Luster gone to?" he asked, a catch in his throat.

"He's went to Melburg after some flour."

"Will he be gone long?"

"I look for him back sometime this evenin'. I cain't know why yo're afeered of Luster, Brother Lazenby. Yo're my paster. He won't hurt you none. He don't keer how much you come out here."

Her voice calmed him momentarily, but he couldn't shake the idea that Luster might return any time.

"You ain't tole him I come out here?" He studied her, uneasily, suspiciously.

"No, I ain't because you asked me no to. But I don't see no harm in hit. I'm always glad to have a preacher in the house and all."

He watched her, all of her, hungrily.

"Yes, Sister Holder, but you must listen to me. You must understand. I can't hold off any longer."

"I can't do what you ask, Brother Lazenby. I'm happy with Luster. They turned me out at Sobby, but I'm still worshippin'. I still have faith in you. God'll understand."

Brother Lazenby's eyebrows drew together. "God can't understand your sinfulness here with Luster Holder. You were not made for a rough life like this, Sister Holder. I want to save you. I've got to save you."

"God He must understand love."

The minister was frantic. "God understands Christian love. Your love ain't Christian. I can't see how a woman like you can love a murderer."

Again she raised her face to him, hopeful trusting.

"Cain't nobody tell who they'll love."

He moved closer to her. "You've got to bring yourself around, Sister Holder. You cain't be lost like this. You've got to leave him and come back to the church while there's yet time."

She shook her head, slowly, sadly. The finality of her refusal maddened him. He took her by the shoulders and looked longingly into her eyes. She never tried to get away from him.

"You must listen to me, Sister Holder," he said hurriedly. Her closeness was almost more than he could stand. He pulled her to him. She turned her head to one side in surprise, her face coloring.

"You cain't know what yo're tryin' to do, Brother Lazenby," she said in faraway tones.

"I do. I do, Sister Holder. I can't pretend any longer. I love you. I've always loved you. I wouldn't have slipped out here if hadn't. I've got to have you. You must make up your mind to leave Luster and go with me. You can't refuse." His voice was choking. Sweat stood on his forehead.

Her words were faint, filled with disappointment. "I couldn't know you was in love with me, Brother Lazenby. I thought you come out here to save me for yore church."

He talked fast, desperately. "It was for you, Sister Holder. I want you. I'm ready to give up the church and everything for you."

"You cain't know what yo're talkin', Brother Lazenby. You got a woman to keer for."

"I ain't. Sudie never meant anything to me. She's like Luster. She don't know love."

"Luster he's good to me. We live like we want to."

The preacher's mind clouded. He bit his lips. "But you ain't been faithful to him, Sister Holder."

"I have, too, Brother Lazenby. I never done nothin' agin him." She looked at him accusingly, hurt. Her mouth drooped.

Brother Lazenby forced himself to carry his accusation further. "Don't everybody at Firbank know how Buck Humphries sneaks out here while Luster's gone? They know how you two have loved behind Luster's back ever since Buck's been big enough to know how to love. I want to save you from all this Godlessness, Sister Holder."

He saw her face go bloodless, ashen. She was white around her mouth like a person when he is deathly sick. She caught at her side and sank to the floor before he could reach her.

He fell on his knees beside her.

"Dossie Bell! For God's sake!"

Her lids fluttered. Her eyes were rolled back to reveal the whites. She whispered, "Buck he's my son." Her head turned to one side and rested against the floor.

He stayed on his knees, unable to get up for some time. When he could bring himself to act, he hurried to the water-bucket for a dipper of water. He wet his handkerchief and sponged her face. She lay pale, motionless. He put his ear to her breast.

Slowly, painfully he staggered back from her.

"My God, she'd dead. I've killed her."

He didn't know how long he stood, stunned, incapable of clear thinking.

He mumbled to himself. "I must get out of here. I mustn't be caught. I've got to save myself. I killed her with dirty words. Nobody must ever know. They can't know or I'm ruined. Luster will murder me in cold blood. She had a heart misery, but who would ever believe me?"

He never knew how he carried her into the big-room and lay her on the bed, or how he crept from the cabin and back through the woods to Firbank.

Since yesterday he had been in a daze. He had tried to keep the memory of the fatal visit from his mind. Luster Holder had led him back to it, forced him to go. The Iron Squire had worn him to a frazzled end in a search for Buck, a search for her son. Everything had closed in on him at once and caused him to realize his own unfitness to say the usual words over her dead body.

It just seemed that everything he'd ever done in life turned back upon him. He could forget all but her death. He was responsible in a great way and wished to lift the secret from his heart, to show these Firbank people he was not afraid to face the truth. He no longer cared what they would think.

The events of the night and morning had determined him to make a clean breast of it. As he repictured the last talk with Dossie Bell, while folks sang around him, he knew he was going to confess everything regardless of the consequences. Despite Firbank and the church, Sudie and his good name, Luster Holder and the threat of death, he was going to tell everything. His life didn't seem so important now as it had prior to yesterday. Nothing seemed so important now. He didn't know what would happen. He didn't think of it.

After he had told the story, he would get away from Firbank as quickly as possible. His work in the hills had finished disastrously. He didn't know where he would go and didn't care just so he got away from the Nation.

And, while silence fell over the perspiring crowd, he told of his unfaithfulness, his love, and his last afternoon with the hill-woman. He told it simply, unhurried, in flat, whispery tones. He talked like a man who knew his life was ruined and was resigned to it. He never looked at Sudie. Only once did he

look at Luster. From outward appearance, the hillman might have been listening to a beautiful sermon
which preached his woman into Heaven.

Brother Lazenby finished and sat down, his body
clammy-cold. The church was very quiet. Then there
was the sound of hissed words which drifted into
rather unguarded talk.

Urfie Pearl Buckner had her mouth by Clemmie
Bean's ear.

"He lived up to what I always thought, Clemmie.
He's a sheep in bear's britches."

"He's shore stepped off into purgatory. I knowed
all the time they was something funny about Buck
Humphries. I'm sorry Granny Blackburn missed-out
on this. She said she'd git here if she could. She had
to drop by home to see Norey a minute."

"Reckin they'll be a lynchin' party started?"

"Naw. Luster Holder'll take keer of ever little
scrimption. He never needed no help in his low life."

Squire Kiler had been asleep when Brother
Lazenby began his confession. Barney Russer awak-
ened him. When the minister concluded, Barney
looked at the Squire and whistled.

Squire Kiler spat a breaking stream of ambeer
into the aisle.

"Hit beats the tar outen nothin' I ever seed," he
growled. "'y God, his shirttail won't hold shucks now.
He hain't got no more chanst than a one-legged man
at a tail kickin'."

Elmer Runnels took the situation in hand. He got up with a songbook opened. Brother Lazenby was seated back of the pulpit stand with his hands clasped in his lap. Elmer knew that folks, although badly worked up over what they had just heard, were anxious to see the body. The confession had made them doubly anxious. They had driven a far way to look at the woman whose name had been on their lips for the last twenty-four hours.

Elmer gave the welcome. "The coffin will be opened as we sing, 'Then We'll Gather at the River.' The right benches will come first and look at the corpse. The middle benches will be next and the left benches last. Then the fambly. Pass out to the grave where we will be dismissed with a prayer by Brother Henley Humphries."

As the song began, folks filed by to see Dossie Bell Holder for the last time: Dossie Bell who had lived with Luster and never married him, the woman whom Brother Lazenby had loved. Curious eyes bored down on the still face of the hill-woman: a face lovely in repose, the lustrous gold-brown hair in a soft silky wave against the pale white forehead, the curved lips bloodless.

The stream of lookers passed in line, some pausing to say words; others crying, their hands to their eyes. A shaking old woman took one glance and set to shouting. She filled the little house with shrieks, throwing her arms around those nearest her and patting backs. All excited talk stopped. Those who had left the church hurried back in.

"Old Bett Coonce is a-throwin' one!"

"The old looney cain't even behave in the presence of the dead!"

The shouting died in one dismal grief-choked moan. Frequently the line was held up as women led their children by to see. One woman stopped with five little fellows trailing her, a baby-boy astried her hip holding tightly to her dress: one by one she lifted them up and out over the casket so they could see the body. She said solemnly to each, "It's Miss Dossie Bell, sugar. She's went to live with Jesus."

At last all had seen. Luster got up and replaced the casket lid. Brother Lazenby hadn't moved from his seat. Squire Kiler walked heavily down the aisle. He and Luster carried the casket out to the grave. The church emptied. People stood in small groups talking, waiting to see what would happen. Many encircled the grave, those on the outside tiptoeing to try to glimpse the coffin as it was lowered. A bouquet of prince's-plumes, which Wurner had brought, lay on the box.

The sun was sinking. Evening light came through the tree-trunks in clouds of red dust, coloring the faces of those who watched. High above, a bank of tiny golden clouds were seared against the unstained blue of the curving sky.

Old man Henley Humphries swayed on his feet, his arms folded. He closed his eyes tightly. His clothes draped laxly on his decrepit body. He held a hickory walking-stick between tremoring hands and leaned over on it to steady himself. His beard, straggling on his sunken chest, seemed to tilt him over.

All who knew him realized they were in for a long prayer. They were anxious to be free to talk. They watched Luster. Brother Lazenby was nowhere to be seen.

Squire Kiler blinked his eyes. "If that ole fool kin pray, I'm Ole Billy hissef," he snarled out loud enough to be heard by all around him.

Humphries prayed through long hot minutes, never heeding the tired sighs and shuffling feet. He said in conclusion:

"Si, much trouble has come into our settlement. The wicked goes unpunished. Si, the innocent hast to suffer. O Lord-God, we're gathered out here to let you know Dossie Bell Holder is dead. Some says she's lost because she never tied up to Luster Holder by man's law. Si, she was shore his in the sight of God. They turned her outen man's church-house, but they couldn't git her outen God's. She was a good woman and thar's no doubt she's in Heaven now lookin' down on the many sinners which condemned her. Si, she done her duty and was a good woman to Luster. What we heerd today proves hit.

"Let yore mercy come down on Luster. Si, hain't no man kin say Dossie Bell and Luster hain't among the best folks which is. Si, she was the finest woman I ever knowed. Amen."

Urfie Pearl and Clemmie talked in subdued tones while Humphries prayed.

"Yonder comes Granny Blackburn, Clemmie. Pore ole soul's missed ever'thing. She'll be plumb burnt up when she hears."

From the roadway into the graveyard Granny Blackburn hobbled, her walking-stick sounding against the packed ground. Her black bonnet flapped in the breeze. She made her way through the crowd.

"You missed a fortune in words, Granny," Clemmie hissed.

"I hain't missed nothin'. Wait'll I git my wind back and I'll fill yore ears so full of news they'll run over and flood yore brains." She wheezed for breath.

"What is hit? Hurry!"

"I left home soon as I could. I come by Kiler's and thought I'd jest drap in and see what was holdin' up Millie. I thought her miseries might of throwed her on her back. I went through the rooms callin' but couldn't start up a soul. I ambled out to the barn. I heerd a groanin'."

She paused to let her words sink in, then continued, "Hit come from the crib. I called, but nobody answered. I pulled myself into the crib and when my eyes could see in the dark, thar was Birdie a-lyin' a-gaspin' on a pile of shucks. She'd jest birthed a boy-baby and was bloody and muddy as air hog slaughtered and half scraped. I hepped her all I could. I think she'll git over hit. I got to rush back. I thought I'd come on out here and tell you'uns. Millie cain't be found nowheres. I got to rush back and keep that god-durned Squar offen Birdie."

Urfie Pearl shook Granny Blackburn's arm. "Who does hit favor, Granny?" she gasped.

"I cain't tell. Hit's nigh black." She turned and hobbled off from them as fast as her withered old legs would carry her.

Folks waited for a long time. Finally they grew impatient and began to leave by twos and threes. They hitched up and started the long drive home. The assemblage thinned out.

Only Luster, the Squire and Sudie remained to watch Wurner and Pud shape-up the mound. Brother Lazenby had not come out to the grave.

Squire Kiler kept yawning. Luster seemed tired and worn by the hours. No one spoke. Sudie looked thoughtfully at the mound.

Silver-and-purple twilight sank gently through the cedars.

"The preacher hain't nowhur's to be seed," the Squire said mockingly. "He sholy must of tuck out fer good. I got to be gittin' on, Luster. The buryin' was a Joe Darter sho. You wantin' to drive back with me, Miss Lazenby?"

Sudie shook her head. Squire Kiler walked to his wagon and team.

Luster and Sudie stood by the grave, wordless, while dusk-dark receded into night. Brother Lazenby did not come. Luster thought of home: The chickens must be fed and barred up. Pattie Pide and the calf, Dimity, must be taken care of. The mules had to be unhitched and fed. It was a long drive to the cabin, but he didn't mind. He could give Cooter and Carnes free reins; they knew the way. He could doze in the wagon.

After the night work was done, he would go to the springhouse and drink the homebrew which he had put there before he left the house. It would be good and cool. He would drink four bottles and go to bed.

He made ready to leave. He became aware of Sudie Lazenby in the darkness near him.

"Are you gonna wait here for the preacher, Miss Lazenby?"

"No," she said with resignation. "He's gone."

Luster's words fell from the dark, calm, decided.

"You come on with me to my cabin. You kin stay there."

He walked toward his wagon. She followed him.

THE END

Excerpt from

THE DEAN'S SECRET

———→✦←———

In the half-light of pre-dawn, the latticed door of a back verandah was pushed gently open and a man descended the icy steps. In the shadow of the shrubbery he paused and looked toward a lighted upper window of the old Georgian colonial house. He sucked in the air with a chill hiss, a wave of warmth running over him. She would be seated before the mirror of her dressing table just as he had left her, her silken hair falling in dark waves to her smooth young shoulders: sitting there to give the last feminine touches to her heavenly beauty before returning to the softness of a bed still warm from recent occupancy.

As the lone light, mellow behind the chintz curtains, went out, he sighed, a great loneliness falling over him. As always when forced to tear himself from the velvety arms and return to the old routine in which so far she could play no open part, an awful feeling of desertion settled cruelly over him and he cursed to hell those things which held him a prisoner from one so young, so beautiful, and so damnably desirable. All left for him now—until the light of safety once more blinked green—was the memory of the stolen hours with her, a memory cold and mocking without her tantalizing nearness, her beautifully solid flesh.

For a minute more he lingered, eyes now directed across the broad open space of the lawn to the far trees. That fringe of water oaks always represented safety to him—the first line of defense on his return to his unassailable sanctuary, empty as it was without his love of loves. His hand shook as he snapped on his cigarette lighter to look at his wrist watch. It was five A.M., Wednesday. The morning was cold and still and bit the nostrils with the odor of frigidity. The November moon, an elongated egg, still hung low in the west, somberly yellow, like embered ashes fanned by a gentle breeze. Every tree and bush was motionless, metallic, unreal, and he could imagine himself on a dead planet as he crept furtively from the depth of shade, and, quickening his pace, hurried toward the woods, trying to hold up his feet from the crackling, ice-hung grass.

In these awful moments, he was always gripped by an old fear, his career hung suspended, and he could see himself discovered, his deception laid bare, and his promising life brought to an ignoble finish—that life he had strived so hard and so honestly to build up so that he might give of the very best of him self-lessly to a world which was weary of an old sickness. A shudder congealed his blood and left him not a part of his heavy woolen suit and overcoat, although he knew for a certainty that the man who could ruin him forever was not due back until late tonight.

Under the trees he mopped icy beads of sweat from his forehead and again thought of the warm bed, the silken comfort against warmer flesh. Yes, it had been hard, cruel, to have to leave it, to real-ize that tonight another would be there in his place, cuddling close the one he so madly loved, drinking deeply from those same parted lips and breathing the sweetness of that same intoxicating perfume, although her mind would be on him alone, each caress dedicated to his memory, as she counted the nights until she could be his once more.

He turned east and walked rapidly over the fro-zen grass, which cracked loudly, vacantly, beneath his thin soles. The campus lights burned dimly at infrequent intervals. The old Gothic buildings of the quadrangle loomed on each side of him without life, as if they were ruins of some ancient university, a ghost university. As he approached a long, stone seat beneath the twisted limbs of a giant elm, he drew up short. Someone, something—dark, indistinguish-able—rose from the seat like a spectre and scurried away, wraithlike, in the half-tone, in a mighty haze.

For a moment terror gripped him and he stayed fixed, in an almost cataleptic state, as his heart hammered ominously. Then he gritted his clicking teeth and shook his head in decisive little shakes to clear it.

He was imagining things. It couldn't be. His eyes were swollen and tired. They were fooling him. He rubbed them vigorously, but when he looked again he saw the figure disappear behind the architectural masses, which were delineated against a low, unreal sky, something spectral, nightmarish and yet curiously real. Who would be abroad at this unholy hour of the morning, when all that breathes should be couched in sleep? In the misty rime of not-night, not-morning, it had been a fantastic, a magical vision, a dream, he was sure. In his highly nervous state, in his feelings of insecurity, his eyes were creating a phantom to haunt him. But in the very creation was a vague foreboding.

He continued on his way and entered a centrally located building. Hard heels resounding hollowly on the tiled floor, he walked down a long dim corridor until he reached a door, on the clouded upper glass of which was printed in bold letters: J. HAROLD MCCARTY, DEAN OF THE FACULTY. He found his keys and opened it.

The Dean's Secret *is a forthcoming novel by Jack Boone.*

THE AUTHOR

J ACK HAPPEL BOONE (1903–1966) was born in Trenton, Tennessee, and raised in Henderson. He earned his Bachelor's and Master's Degrees in English from Vanderbilt University in 1930 and 1931. Boone wrote several short stories both independently and in collaboration with Merle Constiner, including "It Sure Whips Me," "Death Wife," "The Return from Missouri," and "Dossie Bell is Dead." Their work "Big Singing" was recognized as one of the O. Henry Memorial Award Prize Stories of 1932. His only published novel, *Dossie Bell is Dead*, was released in 1939. Boone died in Henderson, Tennessee, in 1966, at the age of sixty-three.

www.ingramcontent.com/pod-product-compliance
Lightning Source LLC
Chambersburg PA
CBHW030410020726
47493CB00003B/1005